Dark Tales for Dark Nights

ISBN: 978-1-932926-21-7

Shadow Dragon Press
9 Mockingbird Hill Rd
Tijeras, New Mexico 87059
info@shadowdragonpress.com
http://www.shadowdragonpress.com/darktales.html

Visit the authors at their website: Mysterious Ink
www.mysteriousink.ca

You can also find them on Facebook at:
Facebook: Mysterious Ink - Pierre C Arseneault & Angella Cormier

Twitter: @AngellaCormier / @PierreCArsent
Email: Angella@MysteriousInk.ca / Pierre@MysteriousInk.ca

Dark Tales for Dark Nights

By

Angella Jacob

&

Pierre C. Arseneault

Albuquerque, New Mexico

**Other titles by
Angella Cormier and Pierre C Arseneault**

Oakwood Island
Oakwood Island: The Awakening

Titles by Pierre C Arseneault

Sleepless Nights
Poplar Falls: The Death of Charlie Baker

Titles by Angella Cormier

A Maiden's Perception: A Collection of Thoughts, Reflections and Poetry

Table of Contents

INTRODUCTION

The stories you are about to read are the results of a collaboration of two people who met because of a love of a great story.

Both having the desire to write for many years, something seemed to be lacking in the task for both of us until a friendship lead to the first collaborative work called "Henry". Having written one short story and already hatching ideas for a few more, the fire was rekindled and Mysterious Ink was forged.

The short story called "Henry" and more are included in this collection. But for now we would like you to sit back, relax and enjoy reading these as much as we loved creating them.

SOMETIMES THEY COME AT NIGHT

The cold water running on my hands and through my fingers was beginning to numb the bout of shakes that had started a short while ago. As night began falling outside, the feelings of worry and anxiety returned when the dreaded darkness began creeping around my cabin in the deep woods.

Years of carpentry had made my large hands powerful with a hammer, yet they trembled in fear now, as they had for so many previous nights. Bent over the sink, I distracted myself for a few moments as I stood washing the last of the vegetables I'd gathered from my garden.

I needed to keep busy in order to distract myself from last night's disturbing events. A heaping serving of stir fry for supper would surely fix my emotional malaise and maybe even comfort me long enough to rest tonight. Relaxation had become a thing of the past in the last few weeks.

With an intent focus, I washed off the dirt from the fresh carrots and chopped them up into long thin diagonal slices. I continued on to wash and prepare the celery, broccoli, cauliflower and a handful of tasty wild mushrooms that I'd foraged from the forest nearby. My pan welcomed these delicious ingredients, making them dance upon its surface in sizzling unison.

Reaching for the sesame sauce, I noticed the red onion, lonely on the counter, it waited to be cut in thin slices and added to the fiesta in the pan. I obliged and for a few moments the knots in my stomach dissipated and I actually felt normal. This didn't last long.

As I picked up the chef's knife from the wooden block on the counter, I saw my own reflection in the shiny wide blade and scared myself. In all my forty-two years of life, never had I seen such deep and dark circles under my eyes. Tired and beat were the words that came to mind. Seemed fitting, I had never before been this scared until this past week. Each night had brought about stranger and more frightening events than the previous. Last night however, had been the one to top all the others. I wondered to myself if they would come back tonight, and if they did, how worse could they become?

It wasn't like I just let them come for me. During one of their first visits, I had tried to escape from the cabin and into the nearby village. They just followed and taunted me with their glowing blood red eyes. Trying to understand what they were saying was pointless. I had screamed out at them several times, demanding to know what they wanted with me. Their only replies had been more of their strange incoherent sounds and rushing towards me as I ran away from them.

I cut the beef into thin strips with the sharp chef's knife. My eyes glazed over as my mind wandered through the haunting events of the recent past. I added the beef strips to the hot pan. The loud and sudden sizzling of the cold meat against the fiery hot temperature made me jump and reinstate the paranoia that had been sitting idle for the past few minutes. A long night was in store, I could sense it before I even sat down in my chair at the kitchen table.

*   *   *

Satisfied with a tasty meal my tired body sank deep in the comfort of my old recliner in the living room. My eyes felt heavy but sleep would not come. I put another log into the wood stove that sat a few feet away on my left. The fire brought about natural warmth, soothing my aching body as well as my mind. I reached down to my side table for something to read and came across the copy of *The Great Gatsby* that my friend Harry had brought over during his last brief and dispiriting visit. Oh, I knew he'd been genuinely concerned about me when he came over, but something in the way his eyes peered through me made me feel like I hadn't convinced him at all.

The last time I had seen Harry had been exactly one week ago today. Early last Sunday morning, I was awoken by the sound of tires crunching gravel. This was a sound I didn't hear very often since I had moved here this summer. Not much traffic came by this deep in the woods, especially not up to my cabin.

Harry had come by to check in on me as he had noticed that I had been quieter than usual and he said I seemed overtired on the job the week prior. We both worked for MacCrombie Construction Ltd, and had known each other since joining the company seventeen years ago. We often went fishing together and occasionally enjoyed a game of pool. Yes, Harry had become one of the very few friends that truly gave a damn about my well-being. When something was up, Harry knew it right away. This was why his visit came as no surprise to me. When my wife had decided to leave me three years ago, Harry had been the only one that I had told.

When our house sold, I bought this cabin on the outskirts of Anchor's Point, a budding town of about fourteen hundred souls. Harry had been one of the few to know where I had relocated. I knew if I could trust someone with my secret, he would be the one. A good friend, I felt sure that I could share my experiences with my buddy in complete confidence.

Unfortunately, my efforts to explain my weariness and worry were met with a pair of disheartened eyes and a look of pity. I simply could not come up with any evidence to support what I was claiming. The scratches I had heard so vividly the night before should have left some kind of markings on the door. There were none. The loud banging sounds made by whatever creature that had stood on the front porch should have left some kind of prints in the dirt surrounding my cabin. No tracks were left behind. A few small tracks, possibly made by raccoons, led off into the woods, but that was all. No, my story just didn't seem to add up to Harry.

As I became insistent on what I had seen and heard, Harry withdrew a bit and suddenly it became clear to me that he thought I was losing my mind. He handed me a few *Outdoors-Man* magazines and a copy of *The Great Gatsby* and suggested I try doing things to keep myself busy. As Harry's Ford pick-up created a cloud of dissipating dirt, I swore to myself then that I would somehow get evidence and prove to my friend that I wasn't going crazy. There really was something in these woods that came alive at night. They were strange and terrifying creatures that looked like they were from another dimension. They were real and I would just have to prove to him that they were.

Now tonight, my eyes finally closing at the end of the first chapter of F. Scott Fitzgerald's classic novel, my head swam in a foaming sea of fatigue and fright, a deep azure wave that slowed down with the hands of my watch, as I felt my body become limp with deep rest.

*   *   *

My heart must have stopped, if even for a fraction of a second, as my eyes flew open to see nothing but the outline of the wood stove standing nearby. It cast off a red hot tint in the small living room, creating long shadows in the neighbouring kitchen.

My sleep had been unexpected, and though my body had needed the rest, it was now fully alert as it heard a long and wailing howl coming from just outside, probably a few yards from the front of the cabin.

I jumped to my feet, the greatness of *Gatsby* now face down on the old floor boards. My socked feet crept ever so lightly towards the kitchen. There came another long howl that seemed longer and much closer than the first. My body now drenched in a cold sweat, my stomach full of knots, I kept my eyes fixed on my front door window.

Past the table, the soft glow of the full moon's rays drenched part of the kitchen floor through the small window above the sink. I tried to stay out of this glow. As dim as it was, I couldn't chance them knowing I was moving in closer. I was determined to catch some kind of evidence tonight.

My feet carefully edged away from the moonlight that formed a puddle on the floor, and I backed my body against the kitchen counter on the far right. My right hand slid along the counter as I moved ever so slowly, keeping my ears open for any indication that they had gotten closer.

Suddenly, just a few feet in front of me, a bright white light shone in through the small window above the sink. The accompanying noise made my ears ring loudly; such was the disturbing level of grinding sound. I instinctively dropped to my knees, now crouched just a few feet off the side of the sink and the source of light that was still pouring in through the window.

On all fours, my eyes were nearly level with the top of the kitchen counter. They fell upon the thirty-two ounce Estwing framing hammer that I'd laid there after work on Friday. I reached up with my right hand and grabbed the tool just as the light disappeared again, as fast as it had arrived. My eyes readjusted to the darkness, but I was already on my feet again before they did.

I moved quickly past the sink and counter and stood just to the right of the front door. My body slightly angled, I silently waited. A few moments passed with nothing but the sound of the strong wind outside. The silence, usually a welcomed thing, made my skin crawl with sheer terror.

Something was out there, I could feel it. It was waiting, staring at the front door. I turned my head slowly to peer over my right shoulder at the kitchen window over the sink. There, batting away long brown wings was the biggest moth I had ever set eyes upon. It was as big as a crow!

It fluttered about, covering at least half the window. It seemed to gain speed as its wings flapped harder and faster. As it hit the window pane, its body emitted an electrical current between the glass and itself, creating a blue glow about it every time it did so. I crouched down to the floor holding the hammer in my right hand. I covered my eyes with my left one as a sudden pain sheared through my temples. Just as I uncovered my eyes and looked at the floor in front of me, I noticed a long shadow in the puddle of moonlight that had beamed down from the front door window.

I stared in shock and held my breath as the shadowy figure stood just outside my door, peering inside my cabin. It began making garbled noises, a mixture of what white noise and an underwater current might sound like if combined. It sounded like it was trying to communicate, but the more I tried to understand what it was saying, the more the creature's speech was broken. A few times I thought I made out a word, but it was so garbled I couldn't be sure. Suddenly, the shadow thing moved away from the front door and the moonlight returned its full beam onto the kitchen floor.

Then, a sudden loud bang came from the side of the cabin, and a long series of shrilling noises came from the same direction. My body shivered uncontrollably in fear. I quickly stood up and looked out the front door. In the driveway danced about half a dozen shadows, their outlines making them easy to spot but from this distance, I couldn't make out their appearance, thankfully. I sunk back down onto the floor, waiting for the perfect time to make my move. I didn't want to chance running outside and being faced with several of these creatures at once. So I patiently waited, crouching down by my counter top and cupboards.

The sudden scratching at my back door made me jump and yelp out in fear. It was louder than I had ever heard it before. It became deafening as it grew louder and louder. Not only was my heart racing at this point, but my ears began to ring as the scratching gave way to gibberish in a language I had never previously heard. The voice was high pitched and divided in two, the scratching itself now morphing into deep penetrating stabs on the back door. Cackles of hideous laughter permeated the living room and drifted to the kitchen, where I stood immobilized in my crouched position. They mocked and taunted me for what felt like hours, until my legs grew tired, but my fright did not.

I sat with my back to the counter, hammer in hand, gripping the handle with whitened knuckles and my eyes wide open. Eventually the scratching faded away and the diabolical voices followed suit. The dimness of the room stood still, and my breathing slowly returned to normal. My body began to relax a bit and the grip I held on the hammer loosened. I closed my eyes for a moment, fatigue carrying my consciousness into a light slumber.

*   *   *

It felt like an eternity had passed when I awoke drenched in a cold sweat, my back against the kitchen cabinets. I held my breath, listening intently in the dark cabin for any strange noises that might have brought me out of my slumber. For the first few moments everything was silent. Then the moment of my deliverance finally came.

As I scanned the windows of my cabin, I felt relief wash over me as I saw nothing out of the ordinary. My body ached and my joints popped as I slowly stood up and grabbed hold of the hammer that had slid away from my hand and onto

9

the cold floorboards. My body felt cold as a shiver passed through it, encircling me as I turned around to face the living room. My eyes grew wide and I gripped the hammer with a powerful hand.

Standing there beside my recliner just in front of the wood stove there stood a large figure. Cloaked in long black rips and layers of flowing darkness, a demon stood at least six feet tall, its eyes glowing a deep pulsing red. It stared intently at me, waiting for me to make the first move.

From deep within me, a strong primal urge, anger and fear mixed together, came up in one swift moment. I screamed as I began running towards the demonic presence that had invaded my home. I ran straight at it, demanding my life back, letting it know that I was taking control again. Just as I reached the dark figure, its eyes glowed bright and it abruptly vanished in a cloud of blackness. The figure now dissipated, I ran straight into the wood stove where the demon had been standing. Searing pain swept up my forearms, the skin charring as I fell onto the stove. I could feel my flesh melting, could smell my skin burning from the contact with the hot metal.

Quickly I got up and looked around the cabin for the demon. Outside, a noise was roaring, the fires of Hell that the demon had unleashed into my world. I stood in the living room, my breathing rapid and my heart racing, but no longer out of fear nor panic. I was now completely infuriated and blinded by rage.

I ran outside, letting out a long guttural scream as I burst out the front door. The cold night air was a brief shock as it cooled off the drops of sweat that had formed on my forehead. I felt a chill running down my back under my drenched T-shirt.

Several of the giant lightning moths had gathered and were flapping their wide brown-spotted wings above my head. At my feet were creatures with glowing red and yellow eyes staring up at me. One of them brushed my leg and began to make strange noises, stepping in between my legs. My left foot came down hard and firm, pinning it on my front porch. It twitched violently underfoot, so I pushed down as hard as I could until I felt bone crunching and I could see an oozing slime coming out of its wide gaping mouth.

I could hear the demon now, raving as it watched me killing its vile offspring of evil. I looked up. In my driveway, I could see the large hole in time and space from which spewed forth the demon. It stood just in front of the bright red glow of the embers of Hell from which it came. It uttered its loud bemoaning and screamed up incantations of which I could make no sense. It came rushing towards me with its long bloodied claws outstretched and ready to tear into me.

Blinded by fury, I mirrored the demon and rushed towards the dark creature of the night, my hammer held up high over my head. I brought it down hard upon the demon, smashing the hammer into its metal-like carapace. I pounded away at it, blow after blow, my fury giving me strength, until the demon was no longer uttering its evil conjurations. Suddenly, a large amount of warm green moss grew over the entity, covering most of it. The glowing red eyes peered dimly from the ground, until they faded out completely as the moss took them over. The earth took back what it spewed forth, and it now lay hidden under a thick coating of moss.

I could still hear the roaring fires of Hell, as the death of the demon had not closed the open gate. The dark shadows seemed to come alive with fresh new evil spirits lurking in every corner. The moths seemed to be approaching me again. I could not fight them all off, there were too many, and my body was tired from the struggle with the demon. I had to escape this now and get help!

The door to the pits of Hell blocked my path up the driveway, so I cut through the forest. I would find the road from there. Running as fast as I could, I felt the huge moths' wings flapping against the back of my neck, which made me run faster still. My legs were tired and my head swam in vertigo but I had to go on...to get help...before more demons came out...couldn't...let them...out.....

*   *   *

Ted Johnson tuned the radio to the local country station that he knew Bill preferred during the drive to work. It was a bright and sunny Monday morning, and Ted was just turning into Bill's gravel driveway. Ted's smile quickly gave way to a quizzical expression when he spotted Harry's pick-up parked there with the driver's side door wide open. The engine was still running too, so whatever had happened Harry must have been in a hurry to not bother turning off the truck or close his door.

Ted pulled up his old Corolla behind the truck and cut the engine. He looked around trying to quickly assess what was going on here. A shiver passed through him, one forewarning him he best be prepared for the worse. The worse imaginable wouldn't even have come close to preparing him for the sight he came upon. He stepped out of the car slowly, his old work boots kicking a few loose gravel stones as he walked up to the parked truck. He reached inside and turned off the ignition. As he was getting back out from the truck, he looked up ahead towards the cabin and had to choke back a gasp.

A few feet in front of the truck was a body, or what was left of it. The head no longer held any shape, having been smashed inwards. It was not even possible to recognize that it had once been a head at all. The body lay in a crimson pool of blood that had seeped into the gravel stones surrounding it. Ted then recognized the corduroy sleeve that was partly uncovered by blood. He was looking at Harry Newman's corpse. With weak and shaking legs, Ted Johnson turned towards his car, and as fast as he possibly could, made his way to it, but not before his breakfast of scrambled eggs and bacon splattered the side of his car door.

*   *   *

Within a few hours, the entire property was crawling with detectives, crime scene investigators, the coroner, search dogs, and the local sheriff. The severity of violence from this very first homicide in Anchor's Point would make it one for the record books in more ways than one. Not only did the officers find Harry Newman's body on the property, but also his dog Chester was found on the front porch, lying dead with several broken bones. A trail of blood led away from Harry's body and into the woods just beyond the driveway.

"We found him Sheriff. He's dead." The young deputy stood holding a bloody hammer in a gloved hand just at the edge of the woods.

"Show me," sighed the Sheriff.

They walked through the woods for about three minutes, along the obvious path that the killer had left. Broken tree branches, bloody footprints and smears of blood on leaves and plants marked the way. They came upon the body of William Prescott, lying on his stomach. The coroner stepped ahead and pronounced the death officially, then turned the body over. Several pieces of grass and leaves stuck to the blood that covered the body's arms, hands and torso. Alongside these bits of nature were other less natural bits: skull fragments, brain matter and skin. Bill was covered with Harry's missing face and distorted head.

The deputy turned and went back to the cabin, not able to stomach what he was seeing for the first time on active duty. The coroner examined the large gash on the body's head.

"I can't officially determine cause of death, that's what the autopsy is for, but my guess is that the fellow tripped on that empty bottle of vodka over there and then came crashing down, hitting his head on this huge rock here." He pointed to a large moss-covered rock that was only a few inches away from the body.

The Sheriff took one look at Bill and then at the coroner and with another sigh replied, "Just bag him up. We got a lot more of this puzzle to put together."

He hiked up his belt a bit just before he set out on the bloody path back to the cabin. When he got back to the cabin, there was a group of four young men talking to the deputy. "Sheriff, these boys claim to have passed by here last night, looking for some, well snacks, but they claim the place was empty when they came up the front door. No lights or anything."

The sheriff opened his mouth, took one look at the disheveled hoodlums with their beady red eyes and sighed loudly. "Go to the station to give your statements boys." With that said the Sheriff returned to his cruiser and radioed for detective Carlyle Walters.

*   *   *

It was later in the day, after the bodies had been removed, that Detective Walters was doing his third walk-around at the scene. He'd closely examined the perimeter of the property, from the body's location, to the pick-up and the front porch. He was now inside the cabin, searching for anything else he may have missed the first few times he'd made his round in here.

They had found some skin remnants on the wood stove, those would have to be analyzed and identified to confirm they were indeed William Prescott's, though matching fresh burn wounds were found on his forearms. The only prints that had been lifted from inside the cabin were those of Bill's, except on the book that had obviously been dropped on the living room floor near the recliner. Harry's prints were found on the book, and his name was inscribed in the front cover. Detective Walters walked slowly back to the kitchen. He peered in the sink. The dishes had been washed, and left to drip dry. A single plate, a steak knife, a fork, a chef's knife, a cutting board and a wok all sat together in the metal "clue" holder.

Detective Walters glanced towards the door as the Sheriff walked in. "Say Sheriff, do you cook a lot?" A small grin started to spread on the detective's face.

"No 'Lyle, I can't say that I do. Martha's the one with the cooking skills at home. What in the world do you ask me that for?" Another sigh escaped him.

Detective Walters walked over to a small dish that was sitting on the counter, between the sink and the stove. "You see Sheriff, my wife Laura insisted that we take a cooking class together just this past summer. She was tired of the same old thing, night after night. She wanted me to take on some of the household responsibilities...enhance my culinary skills and excite our palates...I think is what she said exactly."

The Sheriff crossed his arms and stood broadly in the doorway. "Why are you telling me this?" he asked the detective.

Picking up the small ceramic bowl, Detective Walters smiled broadly now. "One of the classes we took was called 'What not to Eat'. In that class we learned all about the dangers and the side effects of eating natural foods that we find in the most natural of places, like in the forest for example. Mushrooms, being one of the most important foods to be weary of when foraging." Detective Walters picked up a handful of the wild mushrooms in the small ceramic bowl that had been sitting on the counter. He brought them closer to inspect them and said: "Most of these wild mushrooms have a hallucinogenic effect on people. This variety, the Liberty Cap, is no exception."

The Sheriff looked at the bowl of mushrooms and back

at the detective. He took out an evidence bag from his kit near the front door and said to the detective: "I guess we had better bag those for evidence then."

*   *   *

From the kitchen, out the front door, there flew a small brown moth. Down the front porch it went, beyond the gravel driveway, past the truck that was being towed away. It flapped its wings through the bushes and the shrubs. It breezed by the shadows cast in the deepness of these woods, until it grew tired and weary of the long flight. It had been away for a while now, and although the makeshift habitat inside the cabin had been amusing, there was nothing better than returning home.

The moth softly landed on a small mushroom, and peered beyond to several hundred more, carpeting the forest floor.

Yes, how great it was to be back home.

SOUL MATES

The street lamp on Mulberry Lane overlooked the tranquility of the warm summer evening. It cast a soft orange glow on the well manicured lawns, the sidewalks, and the quaint neighbourhood that loved its residents as much as they loved it back. The nights here were always calm and quiet. The most one could expect after sunset was the occasional owl hooting at the chorus of crickets that hid in and around the lilac and hydrangea bushes, common in the area. It was indeed a quaint street in a quiet neighbourhood. Everybody knew their neighbours and took pride in the fact that they were a close-knit community.

Perhaps it was the suddenness of the old man's appearance on the street that caused the street lamp to go out, or perhaps simple coincidence, but the lamp did go dark as soon as the old man staggered aimlessly in the middle of the street, a look of confused stupor on his pale face. His eyes wandered the deserted neighbourhood and then closed for a few moments, his mouth trying to form words that never managed to escape his body.

As his feet struggled to keep him moving forward, Walter stumbled for a few more steps towards the sidewalk. His foot found the edge of the curb, making him lose what little balance he had left, and sent him stumbling down. Both knees hit the cement hard, hands scrapping against the unforgiving surface. His body now lay unconscious and sprawled on the sidewalk. The shadows played on the man's wrinkled face and the night closed in around him as he moaned softly "Rose..."

*   *   *

The two boys were walking home after a night at the movies, horsing around as young boys often do, laughing and playfully heckling each other all the way. As they turned onto Mulberry Lane, Jay stopped abruptly when he saw the man's body crumpled on the sidewalk. He froze in place and grabbed Donnie's sweater, holding him back.

His friend looked at him. Not having seen the body, Donnie got angry and said, "Come on, this is a new hoodie!" Jay's surprised expression told Donnie that something was wrong. His own eyes followed Jay's gaze until they spotted the crumpled thing on the sidewalk. When he realized that what he was looking at was in fact a man's body, he started running towards it.

Jay followed close behind, both boys reaching the man at the same time. They stood over him for a moment, unsure if they were looking at a dead body or a living one. As Jay held back, Donnie bent in closer and looked at the old man's face.

"It's Walter Goodman from up the street. He looks pretty banged up," said Donnie.

Jay looked quickly around, unsure of what he was expecting to find on the lone stretch of street. Most of the houses were dim, their occupants already retired for the evening. "I'm not sure we should stay here, maybe we should go get help." Jay began.

Donnie chuckled to himself and looked up at his friend. "Are you kidding me? Don't you know what this old fart drives? A Rolls-Royce, Jay...and do you know what that means?" Jay's anxious expression quickly morphed into a wide grin as he caught on to Donnie's scheming train of thought. He hunkered down closer to old Mr. Goodman, reaching towards his sweater vest pockets, adding "Hey mister, are you alright?"

Donnie looked up to make sure nobody was watching.

Jay was searching for the antique gold pocket watch that he'd always seen Mr. Goodman wear. When he didn't find it in his vest pockets, he pulled the man from his side onto his back, so he could search his pant pockets. As the man was rolled over, his eyes flew open, and his wrinkled and spotted hand grasped Jay's wrist with a strong hold. The suddenness of his awakening made Jay jump and snatch away his hand.

Mr. Goodman's eyes were not normal looking. They were looking over the two young boys' heads, out to the distant sky above. Donnie nudged his friend and said: "Dude, what's wrong with him? Look at his head!"

Jay leaned closer to the man, trying to get a better look at Walter's head in the darkness. He had a large gash on his forehead, just above his left eyebrow. The cut seemed quite deep, and his blood was still moist on the side of his face. Jay quickly went through his pockets again, while Walter mumbled away, the only discernible word they could make out being "Rose". They knew Rose had been his wife, who had died about two years prior.

"Donnie, he's got nothing on him and he's obviously pretty messed up in the head. Let's get out of here before someone shows up or sees us and thinks we did this to him."

Donnie stood up and smiled broadly. Jay knew that look all too well. "What bright idea did you get now?" he asked his friend.

"Jay, if he's here, that means nobody is at his house." The boys never looked back as they ran down Mulberry Lane towards Mr. Goodman's house.

Lying on the cool sidewalk, Walter's eyes had become wider now, his ramblings faster and still incoherent, though panic was apparent in his weak voice. He managed to turn himself onto his side, his eyes following the boy's feet, pounding the pavement swiftly, moving farther and farther away from him. He reached out his scraped right hand, trying to somehow catch the boys in his weak grip, but it was too late. They were yards away now and in only a few minutes would be on his front lawn. Walter moaned loudly and cried out "Waaait...." as the boy's silhouettes disappeared in the shadows of the night.

*   *   *

The last time the two young boys had seen Walter Goodman had been at The Ketchup Stain Diner about a year and a half earlier. The boys had gone in for a spot to hide out while they skipped classes. Walter had sat a few booths away from them, eating his lunch at his regular booth.

Two waitresses stood behind the counter. Glenda paused from wiping the counter and sighed, "Poor old Walter."

"Why?" asked Abigail. She was a newcomer in town and had not known of Walter's hardships.

Glenda leaned close to Abi and whispered, "Well, he killed his wife six months ago..."

Abigail's eyes grew wide in disbelief. Walter seemed like such a quiet and soft-spoken old man. "What? He killed his wife? Why isn't he in jail if he did?"

Glenda pulled Abi towards the kitchen doors, where she could be sure their voices wouldn't carry into the dining area. "He didn't do it on purpose, of course. Rose had been prescribed a new medication for her arthritis pain and he gave her the wrong dosage." She shook her head, "Poor guy probably couldn't even read the prescription bottle. She slipped into a coma, and died in the hospital about a week later. He hasn't been the same Walter since.

"He used to be so cheery and smiling, came in every morning for a coffee and to read the paper. He still comes in now, but not as often though. When he does manage to get himself out of that house, he talks about Rose like she was still living there with him."

She gave Walter a pitiful glance. "I asked him about it once. I asked if he feels that she is watching over him." Her eyes grew wider as she turned back to Abi. "Well let me tell you he scared the shit out of me that day! He told me that she was still living there with him, still nagging him like when she was alive. Only now he can't leave as often because she forgets where he's gone to and nags him even more!"

Abigail glanced over at Walter, eating his tuna sandwich at his window booth and turned again to Glenda. "Sounds to me like he's losing his mind."

Glenda looked at Walter. The old man returned her glance, nodded and quickly smiled at her. "That's what I'm afraid of Abi, I think he is too."

*　　*　　*

Donnie and Jay reached Mr. Goodman's two storey home only a few moments after leaving Walter on the sidewalk. They glanced around, making sure that no eyes would fall upon their wrongdoings. They ran up the driveway, crouching near the hedges, perfectly lined in a neat row. The night had settled on the property. Long, thin crawling shadows, formed by the tall maple tree branches on the front lawn, danced away on the white siding of the house. The only source of light was the soft glow of the street light.

Jay hurried up the few stairs leading onto the front porch of the house. His mind was set on finding that antique gold watch that Walter had always carried on him, except for tonight. He had decided it would be his, and nothing was going to stop him from getting it.

He crept up while Donnie, still in the driveway, examined the old man's most prized possession, his shiny Rolls-Royce. Donnie noticed that the car had started to show signs of aging. It was still in good condition, but just like Walter, it had lost its luster and shine since Rose's passing. The once polished and waxed silver paint was now a dull grey interspersed with rusting specks. The leather seats that used to be so shiny were now faded and cracked. Donnie remembered the car in its glory days when Mr. Goodman would come to pick up Donnie's father for work at the accounting firm. He remembered his parents talking about the Goodmans and how they had lived a modest life. Their home had been well kept and maintained, and though still in good shape, it now paled in contrast with the newly built and renovated homes on the street.

Donnie was admiring Walter's treasured car, when he heard Jay call to him in a hushed but frantic voice. "Donnie... Come here, quick!" Jay was standing at the front door, nervously peering in. He then looked back at his friend and motioned him to come closer. When Donnie reached the stairs, he asked "How did you open the door so fast?" Jay shook his head and then started "I didn't. It was like this when I got here. Looks like someone already passed Go."

Donnie walked in through the wide open front door. Jay followed close behind. The house was dark, the only light coming from the street lamp that shone through the open door and exposed what looked like the scene of a robbery.

Papers and books were scattered about on the floor. Furnishings looked misplaced, the couch overturned. Even the coat rack was lying on its side, blocking the entryway. Donnie pushed it aside with his right foot, turned quickly and pulled Jay into the house. He peered outside and then swiftly closed the front door. "What if they're still here?" asked Jay.

"They didn't take anything," countered Donnie. "Look, the DVD player is on the floor, and the flat screen TV is still in its spot there too." The house was completely quiet and still showed no evidence that they weren't alone. "Looks like we're good," Donnie whispered. "Just keep your eyes and ears peeled."

Donnie walked over to the living room, being careful not to trip on anything. He examined the disarray and wondered to himself what could possibly have happened.

Jay turned his attention towards the kitchen. The table

had been pushed up against the wall, and a few of the chairs knocked over. As he began to move towards the hallway, something on the counter caught his attention. It was a golden gleam, a soft ticking of time that resonated in his ears. He looked at the pocket watch with greedy eyes, his palms beginning to sweat.

He called out to his friend in the silent house: "Donnie, you should go check upstairs to make sure we're really alone in here." Jay didn't hear what his friend replied. His focus was intent on the watch that seemed to be calling to him from across the kitchen space. As Donnie reached the stairs to the second level, Jay slowly back-tracked to the kitchen counter, smiling.

*   *   *

Walter Goodman remained outstretched on his side, his left hand clutching at his chest. Hearing distant footsteps, he opened his eyes and saw the outline of a jogger coming out of the wooded trail that ran behind the street. The jogger made his way up the street, keeping a steady pace. Gathering up all the energy he had within, Walter lifted his right arm and tried to call out to the man. What came out was a meek whimper. "Help...Rose..."

Walter held onto the hope that this man would see him, call for help and this nightmare to be over. But his hopes were dashed when the man ran up a driveway several houses down, and went back to the normalcy of his own life. Walter closed his eyes once more, his body weakened from the effort. The feeling of hopelessness closed in on him as he drifted in and out of consciousness.

*   *   *

In the kitchen, Jay picked up the gold pocket watch, cold and heavy in his hand. It was heavier than what he expected it would be. He turned it over and read the engraving on the back "Love is Forever....Yours always, Rose (1941)".

Smiling, he slipped the watch into his pocket, letting the chain slowly pass through his fingers, the sensation making him feel important, powerful somehow. He had seen Mr. Goodman's old fingers do the very same thing many times before, as he had put away his watch. Now it was his.

From the corner of his eye something in the living room caught his attention. "Donnie?" he called out, wondering how his friend had returned so quickly from upstairs. A long, low moan came from the living room. Jay, worried that his friend might have come across the vandals that had been there before them, rushed into the living room.

The moaning continued as he walked by the glass-top coffee table next to the overturned couch. With nobody in sight, and the low moan still resonating in the room, Jay began to feel his mouth going dry. He looked in the corners of the room, behind the furnishings, thinking maybe he had missed his friend or someone else in the house. The room was completely empty except for himself and the scattered belongings of the old man.

*   *   *

Upstairs, Donnie found the door to the master bedroom slightly ajar, with still and complete darkness inside. His right hand outstretched, his fingers lightly touched the door. Pushing it forward very slowly, there came a high pitched squealing noise from the hinges as his fingers wrapped around the edge of the white door. He took a step closer, his hand now searching for the light switch on the wall. From inside the room, he heard a soft moaning and froze in place. His eyes darted and searched the darkness. Nothing could be seen from where he stood in the hallway. He held his breath, his ears intent on finding the source of the moaning, but it was too late. Donnie could never have guessed what was about to happen next.

A white cloud-like shape suddenly formed in the middle of the room, illuminating the oak dressers and the large bed that stood nearby. The shape took form and quickly materialized into the wispy outline of an old woman, coming towards Donnie at full speed.

Her mouth was moving, but his ears were ringing with the sound of panic. He stumbled backward, his feet moving quickly to get away from the apparition that was rushing towards him.

About twelve hours earlier, the antique lamp fixture now lying broken on the floor had been hanging on the wall of the Goodman's upstairs hallway. As with the rest of the house, everything that had been stored neatly in its place was now strewn about. Donnie's left foot twisted as the metal fixture disrupted his escape from the translucent being. His arms flung out sideways reflexively to try and regain his balance as his body started to fall backwards.

Had he fallen but a moment sooner, his head may have caught the brunt of the force on the old wooden railing overlooking the living room below. But now his head was far over the railing, his back hitting it with such force that it collapsed under his weight. Sharp wooden pieces and spindles rained down to the first floor. The last thing he saw was the woman's face peering at him as his body smashed hard onto the hardwood flooring in the living room below, two broken spindles jutting out of his stomach and chest.

Death was kind to Donnie, as it didn't linger to make its presence known. It quickly descended upon him and as Jay came running over to his friend Death swiftly went on its way again.

*   *   *

In the hallway upstairs, the wispy apparition started to gain depth. It floated down towards the first floor, calling out "Walter, are you still feeling ill? Should I call the doctor?"

Rose Goodman made her way downstairs, appearing almost herself now, as she had before she'd passed away.

* * *

Earlier that day, Walter Goodman had just started making his afternoon tea. Standing at the stove, he poured boiling water into the two cups sitting on the counter. In a weak and faint voice, Rose asked him if he'd bought milk that morning for their tea.

"Yes dear, I bought milk." Walter replied dryly. He took two tea bags from the white canister on the counter and dropped them in the cups. He brought the tea to the table and sat down, one cup in front of him, the other in front of the empty chair on his right. He glanced up as Rose's spirit whisked about in the kitchen. She reached to open a cupboard, but oblivious to her own demise, her hand went straight through the cupboard and reached for a box of digestive cookies that was not there. "You will have to buy more of these," said Rose. Walter knew full well she was referring to her favourite cookies. "We're almost out." she said as she sat down with the invisible box of cookies she thought she had opened.

"Not a problem dear, I will get more tomorrow." Walter sipped his tea slowly, eyes examining his cup's dark contents, feeling as dark inside as the liquid he was ingesting. Rose was nearly invisible, though he could make out her features. Had he not known her for so many years, he may have not been able to distinguish her face well enough to know that it was really her. She was omnipresent, but at the same time she was near invisible.

Walter felt hopelessness set in as she got up to close the kitchen window. "It's really getting chilly in here, Walter." She tried to push down on the window to close it, but while her hands were moving, the window remained in place. She walked over to the thermostat, small and lifeless fingers nudging at the controls. "We should look into getting a new furnace before winter."

Rose went on as though she had never died. Her life with Walter continued, even after death. Walter closed his eyes and silently wished his wife would find peace in the afterlife, and that he also could find peace knowing she was at rest. As her voice faded, Walter began to feel his heartbeat increase, the pounding of each beat echoing in his ears. Pushing himself away from the table, he got up from his chair, and grabbed his chest as the tightening pressure he felt grew stronger. His knees weak, he stumbled a few steps.

"Walter! Are you alright?!" Rose's voice had been loud! He felt shock pulse along with the pressure within. Her voice had been so weak and frail before. Now it had resounded off the walls of the small kitchen. Walter staggered to the living room, trying to reach the telephone to call for help. Dizzy and weak, he fell to the floor, holding his chest. Rose's ghost rushed over to his side, bumping into the lamp, knocking it over. It fell and hit the TV tray, sending both sprawling across the living room floor, where Walter now lay moaning in pain.

"Noooooo! Walter, hold on dear!" Rose cried. But as she hurried, her foot hit the small table where the phone rested, sending it flying. She turned on her heels, and headed out the living room, passing through a wall where there used to be a door. Her passing through the wall caused a large painting to fall to the floor, hitting Walter on the forehead. A large gash now adorned him just above the left eyebrow, blood oozing out and dripping onto the floor where he lay.

*   *   *

Jay looked down in shock at his friend. Donnie's eyes were as empty of life as was his body. Jay stared at the blood stained spindles jutting out of his friend's stomach and chest. Not able to hold it in any longer, he turned and vomited on the living room floor. From up the stairs, a voice called down for Walter.

Jay jumped to his feet, unsure if he should run or confront whoever just killed his best friend. He swiftly turned toward the stairs just as the apparition arrives at the bottom, confronting him angrily.

"Who are you?! What are you doing in my home!?" Rose screeched at him.

Jay couldn't believe what he was seeing. Rose had passed away over two years ago, how could she be standing so close to him?

With an angry tone, she anxiously called out. "Walter hurry! There's a kid in our house trying to steal from us." Rose's spirit then lurched toward Jay.

In a panic, he turned and began to run. He moved around Donnie's prone form, glancing back at the shape of Rose. He didn't see the telephone on the floor. Tripping over it, he fell hard into the glass-topped coffee table, shattering it. The largest of the shards of glass sliced Jay's neck open from the back of his head. The blood-soaked piece stuck out of his throat, cutting through his windpipe in one long swift movement. Jay gurgled, blood streaming down the corners of his mouth.

Rose's spirit approached him cautiously. She peered down at him, an air of shock set upon her ethereal face. He uttered one last, painful plea to her. With blood spattering the corners of his mouth and upper lip, he mouthed with forced effort "Heeeeeeeelp meeeee."

His face already ashen peered into the eyes of Death. It had come back for yet another visit in the Goodman residence. Glancing at Rose curiously, it continued on its path once it was done with Jay.

*   *   *

Florence had been sleeping soundly in her bed when her cat Tinkerbell came into her bedroom, waking her with unrelenting meowing. "Alright you silly cat, I'm going."

Florence pulls on her terrycloth robe and slides on her slippers. She walks sleepily to the front door opening it to let Tinkerbell out.

Florence does a double take when she sees something on the street in front of her house. Rubbing her eyes a bit she looks again, focusing on the shape that is laying half on the sidewalk and half on the curb. Mumbling could be heard, so she knew it was a person. Quickly closing the door, she walks to her kitchen and grabs the cordless phone from the cradle.

"Clark County Police Department," the operator says.

"There's a drunk passed out in front of my house," Florence says breathlessly.

"OK ma'am. Please give us your address and well send a car right over."

Florence gives the police her address then hangs up the phone. Returning to the bay window she waits for the police to arrive. Florence peers from behind the drapes at the figure sprawled out, obviously drunk and mumbling to himself. A part of her wonders if he might be injured. Perhaps she should step out and check on him? She starts to move away from the window, but a chill walks up her spine. Living alone, the fear washed over her at the thought of putting her vulnerability out there.

She stands solid at the window, arms crossed, one hand holding the drape open. She stood there until flashing red and blue lights illuminated the front of her home. The police cruiser arrived first, and so Florence steps out onto her front porch, safe now that the police were there. The ambulance arrives a few minutes later, and the paramedics began to question the man. Florence feels a pang of regret for not having gone out to check on him. She knew there was no way for her to have known that he was injured or hurt, but she still felt a bit of remorse for assuming the worse. She tentatively walks down her walkway.

One of the police officers comes up to her and with a grim

look says, "I'm Officer Marty, ma'am. Do you have any idea who this man is?" He gestures to the body.

Florence could not see the man's face from where she stands. She walks down to the sidewalk and looks at the injured man, his eyes wide, straining to breathe. "Oh my...," Tears start to run down Florence's face as she informs the officer "Yes, yes. It's Walter Goodman. He's a neighbour who lives just up the street. It's the white house at sixty-seven Mulberry Lane."

Officer Marty nods and looks up the street. He glanced around at the scene around him. The lady in the terrycloth robe held her hands to her mouth, seeming to pray silently. The paramedics were doing everything they could for Mr. Goodman. His partner Doug was standing next to their cruiser, calling the dispatcher.

Officer Marty turns and heads up the street toward the simple white house. Rounding the corner of the driveway, he hears a commotion coming from the paramedics. Marty looks back and sees one of the paramedics frantically running back from the ambulance with a defibrillator. The other paramedic is calling out to Mr. Goodman. "Hang on Walter, we're here for you." Even from this distance, Marty can see that Walter is in cardiac arrest, his eyes rolling back in his head, as he grabs and clutches at his chest.

Officer Marty turns back toward the house and is surprised to see a bright glow coming from the windows. Only a few moments before it had been sitting completely dark and still, he was sure. Officer Marty reaches for his holster and draws out his gun, "What the Hell is going on?"

Marty can hear a paramedic yell out "CLEAR!" As he does so the glow within the house becomes brighter. Another call of "CLEAR!" and the glow from within the house grows a bit brighter. Marty stares in amazement at the house. With each zap of the defibrillator, the brightness within the house becomes stronger. Marty cautiously steps onto the front porch when a sudden burst of light knocks him off his feet, throwing him back onto the grassy patch just beyond the walkway.

Ears ringing Marty shakes his head and blinks away the light, his eyes slowly readjust to the darkness of the night. As he stands up he can hear one of the paramedics say, "He's gone. There's nothing more we can do for him. I just wish we could have gotten to him sooner."

Officer Marty gives the house a cautious glance, then waves Doug over, deciding it's probably best to have backup with him before going in.

*　　*　　*

The two officers cautiously enter the house, Marty holding a long flashlight up to survey the residence. "Man, what the hell happened here?" asked Doug.

It was immediately clear that the home had been vandalized. Debris was scattered everywhere, and furniture strewn about or flipped over. From the threshold Marty looks around and finds the light switch on the wall next to the foyer closet. He flicks it ON, and a flood of overhead light fills the living room and kitchen.

Marty moves slowly through the living room, his eyes falling on the two young boys, bloody and lifeless. "I remember those punks from Juvenile Hall a few years ago."

Marty looks down at Jay's body, seeing an antique pocket watch falling out of the boy's pocket. Gesturing to his partner, Marty says with a grin, "Good old Walter was tougher than we thought. Taking on these two punks by himself."

Doug looks around and replies "Yeah...look at this place, it's completely trashed!" Marty and Doug walk around of the house to make sure nobody else is there, and that everything is secure before heading out to their car to call for the coroner.

As they make their way outside, Marty turns to ask Doug,

"Did you see a bright flash of light earlier when the medics were working on Walter?"

"No I didn't see anything like that," Doug replies. "Why do you ask?" Marty shrugs it off and says "I must have imagined it." Unsure of what he had seen, Marty decides he best keep this to himself.

*   *   *

A few weeks later, The Ketchup Stain waitresses are standing at the counter talking to officers Marty and Doug about Walter Goodman. "I wonder what happened to that nice Rolls-Royce he had," asked Marty.

Glenda wiped down the counter as she explained, "It went up for sale at a decent price, so my husband Charlie snatched it up." She tossed the dish rag over her shoulder as she went on. "It's really been his pride and joy since he got that car. He spends more time with it than he does with me now!" she exclaimed, and they all burst out laughing.

Glenda had a way to turn the most sinister subjects into howls of laughter. But when the laughter ended, she became very serious and she lowered her voice before she went on. "A few days ago, I was filling the coffee pot at the sink and I looked outside to watch Charlie waxing the new paint job on the Rolls. I could of sworn that I seen Walter and Rose sitting in the Rolls. They weren't old and wrinkly like I remembered them though. They were younger, their skin almost glowing. Walter had a full head of hair and Rose was still a red head like when they first bought the car." She smiled nervously before she added "It sure gave me the creeps!"

Abigail popped the bubble she'd made with her gum and smiling, she turned to her coworker, "They say soul mates are forever after all."

Glenda smiled at her and replied, "Maybe you're right Abi...You just may be right." Glenda grabbed a pitcher of water to refill glasses. As she turned away from the counter she noticed a familiar couple sitting at the window booth. The Goodmans turned and smiled at Glenda, then dissolved away into thin air. The pitcher of water she was carrying crashed to the floor as she fainted from seeing the translucent couple vanish.

THE RIVERTON BIGFOOT

Large beads of sweat dripped off the older man's brow on this hot and sticky July afternoon as he began prying up the wooden floor boards, one of many that the pair had plucked off of the house that had been home to the old Dixon couple. The older of the two men, a strong and tall man of fifty-five years, stood up and stretched his aching back for a moment. He looked at the black dumpster that held the pieces of the walls they had torn down earlier in the week. The floor was almost all gone too, and soon Chester Flemming and his nephew Harry would start tackling the beams.

Harry was a forty year old man with dark hair and a muscular build. They both maintained their shape by working construction jobs throughout the spring and summer months. The house they were currently working on was coming down piece by piece, and soon there would only remain the temporary, hollow cavity in the ground that would remind the locals of the house that had stood in the Riverton business district on Main Street.

The crew of two had been hired to demolish the house. Only thirty years old, the home had been in great condition structurally and the only owners of the home had maintained it with obvious pride. This prime location on Main Street however caused their land to be a well sought-after lot. Not many towns had a dead end for a main street, but Riverton did. At the very end of Main Street stood the City Hall. In order to get off Main Street, traffic would have to use the roundabout at the end of the street, and drive down Main a second time. This meant the Dixon house was passed twice, which made it a prime location for any business. Merle and Molly Dixon had been turning down offers to sell from eager business developers for several years. After Merle's passing though, an aging Molly decided it was time to move into a smaller place of her own.

Harry and Chester had been given a month to tear the place down. They decided to spare the businesses on Main Street the noise of heavy equipment and so they went to work the old-fashioned way. They could salvage anything they wanted this way also, which turned out to be quite a bit, as the house was still in good shape. There was nothing much left of the house today though.

Chester glanced at his nephew as he wiped the sweat from his brow with his gloved left hand, leaving a streak of dust where the sweat had been and said, "Hey Junior, sorry about your dad. It's too bad he had to go that way."

Harry Junior looked over to his uncle and could see real sympathy in his eyes. "Yeah, he didn't last long after the doc told him the news that he had cancer," replied Harry. "We're gonna have to take a few days off, the wake is the day after tomorrow." Harry took off his dirty work gloves and reached for his bottle of water on the dusty wood floor.

"Of course, we're ahead of schedule anyhow. There's no problem there." Chester replied. He started pulling and prying off the floorboards once more and continued on. "You realize the wake is gonna be a bit crazy, right?"

Harry threw a long piece of wood on top of the large pile they had amassed in one corner of the house. He turned and faced his uncle. "Oh I know. Dad's been famous here for the last thirty years."

Chester grinned a bit. "That's an understatement. He put this place on the map!" He continued to work as he went on "Everyone in town thought he was crazy, telling people about the huge footprints he had seen by Bear Creek. I wish I would have been here to see it for myself. Makes it hard to believe when you don't see it with your own eyes, ya know?" Harry nodded, his face growing more serious and he began recounting his memories of how his father had put a permanent mark on the town of Riverton.

"They found even bigger footprints in old Lester's garden," Harry said. "I remember it like it was yesterday. I was playing right here at the construction site of this very house actually, now that I think back. Like any other ten year old, I ran over to Lester's as soon as I heard about the commotion over there.

"He'd been tilling his garden when he came across a hole that had been dug up in the middle of it all. When he went about examining it, he saw a pair of large footprints there. One print alone must have been about eighteen inches long and twelve across. They took pictures but by then people had trampled about to look at the hole in the ground and so the prints were partially destroyed. Lester had erased all the other prints with his tiller, never noticing they were there 'til he came across the hole. He must have been half drunk again, the old fool!"

Harry and Chester continued working as they talked about Harry Senior and the wild stories that had began spreading that summer thirty years prior. Harry Senior had been the first to find evidence of some kind of creature bearing these large prints in the Riverton community, and because of this he had become a celebrity for a few weeks. His fifteen minutes of fame were cut short when the skeptics starting talking and arguing the validity of his claims. Soon Harry Senior had been labelled crazy. This in turn sparked a frenzy in Harry's father, as he knew what he had seen and was determined to find proof.

Across town, on the same day Harry Senior had made his discovery, Charlie Bryerson's old Pontiac had been found with a huge dent adorning the hood. The front suspension was destroyed to the point that the oil pan was touching the ground. Along the edge of the driveway there stood a row of flowerbeds in a multitude of bright colours. It was below the cascading petals in the soft earthen soil that a partial foot print was embedded. Several people passed by the spot that day, but with only a partial print and none knowing any better, nobody noticed the outline for what it really was.

On that day Riverton became famous, all thanks to Harry Flemming Senior. He had claimed to have seen several sizes of prints, all larger than a human could ever possibly make, but he'd been able to discern three distinct sizes of prints. These claims began a string of sightings from locals and tourists alike in the following months, the latter flocking to Riverton for the next few months in an effort to see the now famous Riverton Bigfoot. Most of the sightings turned out to be bogus claims from people wanting in on the action.

Harry Senior had been interviewed by the local and regional news reporters. Together they had spent a few hours filming the spot where he'd claimed to have found the prints. They asked him to recall every detail he possibly could of what he had seen. Many people had wanted the same attention and so the masses came to Riverton. Even a few souvenir stands popped up around town, selling Riverton Bigfoot T-shirts and baseball caps. This had all started around the end of May, and by September things had finally started to get back to normal in town.

December of that year had been bitter and cold, leaving its frozen grip on Riverton soil. Though there had not been a single snowfall yet, and no more footprints had been seen since earlier on in Spring that year, most of the town was convinced that Glendale Hicks's farm had been visited by the Riverton Bigfoot. The family dog had been found dead, his body distorted in an unnatural fashion, his limbs and ribs crushed to bits. The veterinarian told the family that whatever had hit him was big and had done so with an incredible force. The sturdy fence was still standing but yet three sheep were missing from their property. The only thing the Hicks family had found was a small patch of light brown fur on one of the barbs on the fence.

Two more sheep would disappear that winter, both during an intense snow storm in February. This time the sheep were taken from inside the barn. One single footprint was perfectly formed in a patch of snow near the door of the barn. By the time old Glen got his wife to dig out their Polaroid camera, the snow had melted from the heat coming from the barn's open door. The evidence was gone by the time Glen's wife had found the camera. The stories surrounding all these events fed the ones that had started earlier that year. The stories grew and morphed into tales of grandeur by some less than believable locals and vacationers. Indeed that year the legend of the Riverton Bigfoot was born.

* * *

Thirty years later, Riverton still held onto the legend as much as it had held onto the surrounding woods that encased the town. Just beyond city hall, down past the first large patch of woods behind the municipal buildings, there was a very small and odd-looking clearing in the woods. It was shaped in a circular pattern, a thick ring of trees lining the clearing. Had it not been for the differing height of trees in the circle, one might have thought the trees had been deliberately planted that way. The area held a few cool spots where the shade trapped the wind in its grip.

It was in this clearing that a creature squatted, long brown fur covering its entire body. It sat and waited in a heavy silence, its presence cloaked by the shadows of the forest. It had grown restless, hunger overcoming its every waking thought. Some would have said it looked like an ape, but its features had a human-like appeal, although this creature was clearly not a man.

Even as it squatted on the ground its head would be

taller than most men. Stillness surrounded the clearing and centered itself on the creature. It sat completely still, its shallow breathing as quiet as the air that moved in and out of its huge lungs. It stayed there crouched in the same position for a very long time, its innate fury intact.

Suddenly, its head twisted to one side as if some sound had caught its attention while its eyes fixed on a distant spot in the woods. In an instant, the creature had crossed the clearing, a blur of speed and agility like none had ever seen before, nor would see coming. Its massive legs crossed the clearing in the direction of the deer it had so aptly heard coming from such a great distance with its sensitive hearing. It wrapped one of its large hands around the deer's neck and picked it up several feet off the ground. The deer's legs kicked and bucked as it struggled to breathe, its windpipe crushed in the creature's murderous grip. A loud snapping then a cracking sound echoed in the forest and the deer was suddenly hanging limp and dead in the creature's hand.

The air carried a lingering scent that the beast picked up at once. It dropped the deer to the ground and spun around, its eyes fixating upon what it already knew would be staring back. The familiar and sickening stench of man had permeated its nostrils moments before, and now there stood before it the small weakling of a man.

John Murray stood frozen in fear, staring at this eight foot tall hairy, man-like creature. It had just killed the deer that he had been stalking for the last hour. The beast had snapped the animal's neck with one massive hand in a swift motion. The creature now stood before him and began snarling, exposing pointy and sharp teeth dripping with foul smelling saliva. Even from this distance he could smell the creature, a pungent odour coming from the beast and infecting his own nostrils, making his stomach churn from both fear and repulsion.

His rifle blasted out one explosive shot before the creature reached him. John would never know if he hit it or not. It had reached out for John and grabbed his head in one single hand, crushing his skull instantly, the bits and fragments mixing in with the pulped goulash that just moments prior had been John's brain. Every bird and small mammal flew or ran away at that moment when they heard the guttural roar echoing through the forest. The creature hoisted John's limp body with a single hand and threw him over its massive shoulder. It picked up the deer with its other hand and headed back towards the clearing, returning as quietly as it had arrived. It would dine on raw meat again tonight, as it had been doing for so many years in Riverton.

*　　*　　*

It was the day before the wake. Harry and Chester had been working all morning. They were done tearing apart the floors and had hauled in some equipment to start demolishing the basement. They took a longer lunch that day and talked about Harry Senior again.

"You know your dad was still convinced, even 'til he took his last breath, that Bigfoot was still in the woods on the outskirts of town." Chester offered a sincere smile to his nephew, his right hand lifting up his baseball cap as he scratched his sweaty forehead.

"Oh I know. His obsession grew stronger as time went on. He never could let go of that thing. Did you believe his stories uncle Chester?" Harry had often wondered to himself if he was a bad son for not believing. His uncle's reply came as a comfort to this worry.

Chester put his right hand on his nephew's shoulder and replied "One might as well believe in aliens or the tooth fairy. Bigfoot is just a legend son, you know that." He squeezed Harry's shoulder before he chuckled a bit. "Now let's get back at it for a little while so we can go home and get some rest for the funeral home tomorrow. I have a feeling it's gonna be a long day." Not long after, the area buzzed to the sound of Harry's jackhammer pounding on the Dixon house basement floor.

*   *   *

Instinct had been a friend to the beast in the woods that adorned the outskirts of Riverton. It remembered the passing of the two others of its kind that had been living in these woods for many years. The two others were much bigger than it had been when they passed away. It was by using its own adaptability that had allowed it to survive alone in this unfamiliar wilderness. Its kind, unlike man, would never fall into deep depression over living such a lonely and solitary life, spending each sombre day merely surviving by instinct alone. Its kind simply grew accustomed to it and adapted.

Its hunger was the one thing that its lonely life had revolved around for the past thirteen years. It had started struggling alone since the death of the others of its kind, struggling for survival in this small community. It searched for food, stalking the woods, crouching and hiding, allowing its superior senses to pick up on any approaching prey before capturing it and taking it back to the clearing where it would feed on its kill. It was not always an easy task to go undetected by the pesky man creatures. They were the ones to watch for, as they had their weapons and their technology and although its strength and speed would be no match against any man, its body was no match against their metal and machines. It had grown to loath man during its years on Riverton soil.

Hunger had been its one focus, its only need and want. It had consumed most of the small deer in one day. The creature, large and powerful, had a massive appetite and only filled itself with meat. It was now working on consuming its last kill. John Murray had not been a very big man and the beast did not care very much for man flesh. It had eaten its fair share of man in the past years, but it would rather have had another sheep. It was getting difficult to keep satiated, as wildlife was getting scarce once more. There had been days when all it had to eat was a rabbit or two.

Today it would have a good meal though, gorging on both the deer and the man. When it fed it ate nearly everything except the bones, claws, hooves, and teeth of a kill. Its kind left nothing else, it ate the organs and the flesh as well. Once done with the remnants of what had once been John Murray, the creature flung the skeletal remains on top of a giant pile of clean bones of varying sizes and types of animals. There were bones of deer, moose, bear, rabbit, fox, coyote, man, sheep, cow, pig, and nearly every other wild or farm animal that it could sink its teeth into in order to feed its large appetite. All these animals had met the same fate and had become another meal for the giant razor toothed creature known locally as the Riverton Bigfoot.

*   *   *

The concrete floor of the old Dixon house basement was breaking up bit by bit, proving to be much more difficult than Harry and Chester had originally thought it would be. They had spent all day chipping away at it but still progress was slow. They had assumed by looking at all the imperfections in the floor that it would be easy, but the spacing between each of the rebar was so small that it proved to be an arduous task.

By late afternoon their muscles ached and they were about to call it a day when Harry walked to the middle of the room. Here he noticed a few imperfections in the concrete and looked at these closely. He wondered how the floor had passed inspection with such shady workmanship. A piece of rebar was even partly showing through the top of the floor. As Chester continued on with the jackhammer, a sudden crack formed from the middle of the basement and outwardly on each side, reaching the far end of the basement walls. A loud popping sound was heard over the jackhammer as the fissure spread out in the concrete. Chester turned off the machinery and joined Harry in the middle of the room to examine the spot where the crack had first sprouted.

"Well ain't that strange," said Chester looking at the spot.

"It looks as though there was no rebar here at all," said Harry.

Chester turned and picked up the sledge hammer that was sitting on the dusty and crumbling floor. He brought it down hard and a large chunk of concrete broke off and exposed rebar underneath. The rebar was bent downwards for some reason, leaving a wide gap in the center. Chester continued on with the sledge hammer, large pieces of concrete falling away, revealing more of this strange formation of rebar, forming a circular pattern.

Once the section was completely exposed, the strangest thing came into view. A large metal ring had been buried in the concrete before it had hardened. Somehow the concrete now just fell away from it as if it couldn't adhere to it.

"What would be the purpose of something like this anyway?" asked Chester while holding up the ring.

"I don't know. Maybe it was to be part of a drain of some sort," replied Harry as he examined the smoothness of the strange ring.

"All I know is I've never seen rebar like that before. No wonder the floor was cracked." He picked up the sledgehammer, placed it against the basement wall and said, "Well I say it's quittin' time for today. Let's get some rest for your father's funeral tomorrow."

They went up the ladder to the ground above the open air basement. The house demolition was nearing completion. As they walked to Harry's truck and climbed in, Chester rolled down his window as he asked Harry: "How's Becky holding up?"

Rebecca and Harry Junior had been married for twelve years now. "She's doing OK. She never really understood dad's obsession with the Riverton Bigfoot. They grew apart over the years as she thought it was nothing but a waste of time to be chasing legends."

Chester opened his lunch box and took out a can of soda. As he opened it he turned his head toward his nephew and said "Well you best get home to her then and get some rest tonight. Just drop me off at Frankie's. I could use a few cold ones." They drove down Main Street talking about the wake that would take place the next day.

*   *   *

Across town, the beast was wandering further away from the clearing as it began searching for its next meal. It had been a day and a half since it had last fed. Hunger had begun creeping into its gut earlier that day. The beast squatted down and listened for the sounds of prey that would eventually come. Its large body almost doubled as that of a bear, crouched down on all fours. As the sun's rays were peering through the thickness of the trees in the forest, the beast reared its head and stood upright in an instant, a grunt escaping its throat. It appeared spooked, something uncommon for this massive creature to experience.

Standing frozen with apparent confusion, it looked off in the distance, listening for the sound it had heard. It bolted as fast as a deer, its legs making long and powerful strides back towards the clearing. It ran as fast as it could, not a single worry of being spotted by the pesky men it had been so careful to avoid all these years.

When it reached the clearing, it ran through the thick brush surrounding it, and off to one side where the evergreens and bushes were overgrown. The beast slowed down to a walk and its large hands parted the trees, slipping through these with ease. It spent a few moments in this thick vegetation before emerging again, clutching a plain metallic object in both hands.

The object appeared to have no seams and the rounded edges shaped it into a distinctive metal cube. As the creature held the box in both hands, it dropped to his knees and sat still, waiting, eyes fixated on it.

A few moments later, a faint beep was heard coming from the box. A look of human-like desperation spread across the creature's face. The box emitted another soft beeping sound a few minutes later, and the creature bolted upright. Its eight foot tall frame casting a long shadow all the way to end of the clearing as the setting sun cast its light through the trees.

As the beast held the box close to its chest, it began walking slowly at first, appearing unsure of which direction to take. As the beeping continued it kept walking, the look of desperation still plastered across its monstrous face.

*   *   *

The Riverton Watering Hole was the local bar where some of the townsfolk would converge after work to enjoy a few brews and share stories and laughs. Chester sat on the bar stool still in his work clothes. He took a few swigs of the cold beer that Frank the bartender had just set down in front of him and then continued telling Frank and a few of the other patrons about the metal ring they had found in the cement at the house. He looked up and said to Frank "It was the strangest thing I've ever seen!' Was a shiny thing considering it spent thirty years in concrete."

Thomas, sitting on the stool at the other end of the bar said, "I think you're lying Chet." Thomas was a skeptic and naysayer, especially when it came to stories from Flemming men. "Why don't you show us this here shiny metal ring?"

Chester chugged down the rest of his beer before he replied. "It's getting dark now, but we can go see it in the morning if ya really need to see it." Chester shot a look towards Thomas.

Thomas got up and walked over to him. He crossed his arms as Chester turned on his bar stool to face him. Thomas continued "Such a liar, just like your brother Harry always was."

Now Chester knew Thomas was only talking this way to anger and get a rise from him. He figured Thomas wouldn't let it go, and he knew what he said was true, so he took up the offer. "Fine then, let's go."

Chester got up and led Thomas outside, his breath quickening from the anger that had started to well up from deep within. Chester got in with Thomas and they drove down the street to the old Dixon house. Thomas grabbed a flashlight from the back of his truck's cargo box and handed it over to Chester, who was now waiting by the ladder. He descended down to the basement; Thomas followed.

"It's right over there." Chester exclaimed as he swept the ray of light to the centre of the basement floor. They walked over to it and Chester picked up the metallic ring, which was a good three inches thick and about two feet in diameter. He held it up and said "Told ya."

The beam from the flashlight shone off of the metal, as shiny as if it had just been polished. Thomas took the flashlight from Chester before he said "What the heck is that?"

Chester replied, "We found it right there where those weird bends in the rebar were."

When Chester turned to show the other man, he noticed an odd faint glow coming from the hole below the crumbling concrete they had started to remove. "What the hell..." Chester was intrigued by the glow and never noticed the widening of Thomas's eyes.

"Ch...Ch...Chester!!" said Thomas as he tugged on his arm. Chester turned around again and followed Thomas's wide stare to a huge silhouette standing just at the edge of the basement, where the ladder stood tall. It was clear that it was no man casting the shadow. No man could be that tall.

"Holy mother of God!" exclaimed Chester, as he stumbled back a few steps.

The creature jumped down onto the basement floor, making it shake a little as it landed on its two massive feet. Debris from the side walls of the foundation crumbled down and hit the floor with small resonating echoes.

Thomas cast the flashlight upwards and pointed it directly at the creature, his hand trembling with fear. Chester, mustering up all his courage, stepped towards the wall and picked up the sledgehammer. He hoisted it up in self-defense.

The creature swatted away the flashlight in Thomas's hand. It swatted it so hard that Thomas's right arm tore off at the shoulder. Thomas shrieked for only an instant as the creature swatted again with the same hand, back handing Thomas in the head. This removed his head clean from his body, and it rolled off somewhere in the darkness of one of the basement corners while the body stumbled forward and collapsed. Chester stood frozen in place, his eyes locked on the gruesome scene, trembling in fear. The smell of urine filled the air as the fear he felt overcame his senses and he lost control of his beer-filled bladder.

The creature walked over to the glowing pile of rubble in the centre of the floor. It did not seem interested in Chester at all, removing pieces of the rubble one by one, until a glowing orb came into view. As the beast busied itself with the glowing object, Chester sneaked up behind him, poised to strike it with the sledgehammer.

The creature, its senses sharp and accurate, brought out a giant arm and swung it backwards without even a glance and Chester was sent flying across the basement. His body smashed against the cement wall with brute force, the sound of breaking bones filling the silent summer air. Chester slumped to the floor, dead before his body slouched against the concrete. The beast reached into the hole in the floor and with two massive hands it pulled out a faintly glowing white orb. The orb pulsated as if alive.

The creature picked up the metal ring and in two steps it leapt clear out of the basement, running at an incredible speed through the peaceful streets. It ran past Wally's Hardware Store and then out in the field behind the store. It ran as fast as it could towards the woods just beyond these fields. Once it reached the woods, it kept running until it reached the clearing. Running straight into the thick brush, the glowing of the orb brightened. The trees and evergreens were illuminated by the glow, casting strange shadows all around the forested area.

The unusual shadows were no match for the displacement of the peculiar looking triangular shaped craft that stood on three legs. The shiny metal that covered the craft perfectly matched the metal of the ring that the creature had looped around its arm as it ran. The hairy creature swiftly crouched underneath the craft. Its giant hands grasping the orb and pushed it upwards into a hole in the craft's underside.

As the creature let go of the orb, it seemed to be suspended in midair. The creature placed the ring over the orb and began twisting it into place. A snap-like locking sound came about and at that very instant the craft seemed to come alive. All the seams in the craft glowed faintly, emitting a soft white light from every line and fissure. Without hesitation, the creature stepped out from the underside of the ship and proceeded to climb into an opening on the side. As soon as the creature had boarded the craft, the doorway closed, sealing itself shut. A few brief moments later the ship shot upwards so quickly that anyone nearby would have easily mistaken it for a flash of summer lightning.

*   *   *

Harry put his arm around his wife's shoulders as they sat on their beige couch, still wearing the dark attire they wore for Harry Senior's funeral a few hours prior. Susan turned on the TV and tuned it to the local news.

"I can't believe I just buried my dad and now I have to bury my uncle too." He looked at his wife with tired eyes. He pulled her closer and rubbed her shoulder to comfort her. "What did the Sheriff say?" she asked. "Do they have any leads on who killed Chester and Thomas?"

Harry brushed a strand of her blonde hair off her forehead. "Not yet. If they do they're not sharing with the rest of us anyways. When I went to identify the body they seemed pretty baffled as to who would do something this gruesome in Riverton. My guess is that it was probably an outsider. Hey there it is, turn it up a bit." Susan reached for the remote and turned up the volume as the reporter began her news report.

"Amanda Lessante here, reporting from Riverton. The small town was first saddened by the passing of a well-known local man but is now in shock at the news of two gruesome murders that took place less than twenty-four hours ago in this small, close-knit community. Harry Flemming Senior was a man known by many, near and far. It was just about thirty years ago that the local man put Riverton on the map when he claimed to have found evidence of not one, but multiple creatures that became known as the Riverton Bigfoot."

Susan sighed heavily and rolled her eyes at Harry. "Of course they are going to mention that. Why can't they just let him rest in peace without bringing up the monsters?" Harry shrugged at this and turned up the volume a bit more as the TV now showed a very large foot print in soft gravel. Harry recognized the hardware store from the red and white signage on the building. The reporter continued on.

"Fanatics of the Riverton Bigfoot legend that were in town for Mr. Flemming's funeral came across what they claim to be a footprint that could have only been made by a very large, two legged creature." On screen, a man dressed in a camouflage jacket and steel toed boots measured the footprint.

"That there's a Bigfoot print and ain't no one that'll tell me different. See how big it is and how wide the stride woulda been? There ain't no man in Riverton that woulda been able to do that, least not that I know of." Wally, the hardware store owner stood beside the print and the man with the measuring tape. He stood over the print, hands on his hips while the reporter brought the microphone to him.

"After Al here found the print, I looked over the video footage from my security tapes and I think I might have something."

Amanda Lessante raised an eyebrow. "What did you find, exactly?"

Wally pointed to the video camera that was mounted on the side of the old building. "Well, the quality ain't there, but you can definitely make out the outline of a very big creature running past the building here in that direction. It's hard to say exactly what it is but it sure ain't human, that's for darn sure!"

"Let's take a look at what the video shows and you can decide for yourself what to make of it," said the reporter. The grainy video that came onscreen showed a bright glow in the centre and the barely visible outline of a large, possibly two legged silhouette running past the store.

"Upon hearing about the murders from witnesses at the crime scene, I interviewed the local police department and here is what they had to say about the murders." Harry turned up the volume again as Susan placed her head against her husband's shoulder. They listened to Sheriff O'Keefe onscreen.

"We can confirm that two bodies were discovered at a house that was partway through demolition. Foul play is definitely suspected, as the scene did show a clear indication of struggle. Excessive force and violence also played a part in the homicides. We have no suspects as of yet. That's all I'm at liberty to say at this point. Thank you." The Sheriff stepped away from the reporter as she turned to face the camera.

"One thing that is certain is the uncertainty of what exactly happened last night in Riverton. Locals and visitors alike have been sharing their views of what they believe might have happened. Let's listen to what some of them had to say."

The image on the screen showed a close-up of a man dressed in coveralls and a ball cap with the caption onscreen reading "Local farmer believes Bigfoot stories". The man pointed to his barn and recounted his experience. "All I know is that something kept coming to my farm to steal some of my sheep at night, both in winter and summer. I suspected a coyote until I found a rather large print myself once, in the snow. There is no creature known to this area with a print that size, and that's that. I know what I found and that's all that matters to me."

Susan shook her head, disgusted. "Why do they encourage this? I thought this whole thing would just go away once we buried your dad. Now it's just starting all over again. I've seen enough." She started to get up but when a man wearing a business suit and a very serious look appeared on screen she sat down again and listened. This time the caption read "Skeptic needs solid proof."

"Having disproved several cases of alleged Bigfoot or Sasquatch sightings, this one does not seem to hold any more proof than any other. One man's storytelling skills stirs the rumour mill and eventually the rumours become so called "facts", with nothing more than part of a print in some dirt.

Show me some DNA. Genetic proof that this is a species that has never been documented by scientists and then we might have something to go on. This is simply another attempt to re-stir the rumour pot in my professional opinion. Nothing more than an attempt of a cruel last joke at the expense of a man who was set on making this hoax of a story about Bigfoot appear real."

Susan sighed and got up from the couch. Harry watched her walk away. He was saddened by her apparent disappointment that all this negative attention attached to their family was once more her reality. Harry got up to turn off the television but listened to the last part of the news report. It was an older couple wearing Bigfoot souvenir T-shirts and caps. The woman spoke while the man nodded his approval.

"Jerry and I camped out in the woods here while on a road trip back in the day when Mr. Flemming first recounted his findings. We felt something in those woods that night and heard very strange noises coming from the dark. I knew there was something there. I could feel it watching me that night. We come back every year but we don't stay near the woods. Not since that night. Bigfoot is real! One day everyone will believe!"

The reporter returned to the screen, microphone in hand. "The Riverton Bigfoot. Is it a hoax or is it real? A town divided over this question for decades and still appears to be divided today. Perhaps one day the legend will be proven to be factual. Until then, this is Amanda Lessante, reporting from the town of Riverton."

Harry turned off the television and walked upstairs to comfort his grieving wife.

*   *   *

In the clearing the large pile of bones began tumbling down as a few wild dogs foraged the remnants for a tasty treat. They rummaged through the bones, casting aside the ones they deemed unfit for their snack. As they reached partway through the pile, one of the dogs pulled out a large femur, at least four feet long, it had a stark white brightness compared to the rest of the bones. Never before had it feasted on this sort of bone. The other dog quickly joined in the hunt to pull out the bones of two unnaturally large skeletal remains from the pile. The teeth marks they left in these bones would soon cover up the other bite marks left behind by their first predator so many years prior. One of the dogs ran off with a large misshapen skull. This was their first finding, but surely not their last.

They would return to the pile many times over the following months, along with several other wild animals, until the pile of bones became but a shadow of a memory of what had once fed in the clearing of these woods.

MAYHEM AT THE HENDERSONS

The morning dew wept, sliding down the grass blades as the rising sun crept upwards over the field at the Henderson's place. The spring sunrise showered the new day with its prospects and promises of renewed bounty at the farm.

From outside the old barn, the sunlight inched upwards, creating a golden facade which contrasted well with the red exterior. From inside the barn, however, the sun's rays also brought about a disturbing clarity to the bloody crimson covering the dirt floor. The rays peered through the thin slits of the wooden walls, and cast down a plentiful row of brightness upon the bloodied boots of the man.

Cowering in the far corner of the barn, Alice tried to hide behind some old machinery, her head dizzy with the events that had unfolded before her eyes. The sadistic man had held them all captive in the old barn for two days, and had just now started to kill them off, one by one. Their attempts to escape the night before had failed. The door would not open and they were trapped inside the decrepit barn overnight.

The man had come back just before the sun started to rise. Careful not to rouse them, he'd entered in the still dark space where he'd kept them. Alice wanted to erase the visions that were now ingrained in her mind, but the horror of what she had witnessed would not leave her. The man first attacked her good friend Wendy. She hadn't had a chance to cry out as he had brought down his axe upon her, the blood running down the handle and onto his boots.

Then her friend Janet had been next. Her screams carried the fear and the anguish of what they had all felt. She had struggled against the powerful grip of the man's large hands. She had tried to escape him, but her struggles had been pointless. His axe carried her death on the sharp blade, her soul disappearing into his wild and hungry eyes. Those eyes had seemed hungry for their blood and held reflections of his sick, demented mind.

Alice felt fear, but mostly she felt saddened knowing that the end was drawing near for her own soul. As he brought down the axe for a moment, it thumped against his boot, a sickening and morbid reminder of the power it held over them all. His eyes peered at Alice, still in the corner, trying to avoid being seen by the monstrous man.

He walked over to where she crouched, close to the dirt, her eyes avoiding his own. He grabbed her neck with one massive hand, and pulled her towards the middle of the barn, where death waited with a mocking grin. She clawed at his arms, and tried to bite the hand that held her down. For a brief moment she managed to squirm away, but when he took hold of her once more, she knew the end was drawing near. He held her head with his foot now, his dirty boot pressing down on her hard. Her wide eyes felt the shadow of his rising arms over her soon to be lifeless body. It seemed that time stood still, each second lasting longer than the one before as she waited for the one final blow to end this nightmare.

She felt the shadow slither away from her and at the same time her eyes caught the glint of the blade reflected in the sun. It bounced off of the old broken window directly across from her. The bright reflection of the sunlight shone directly into her eyes, and Alice embraced this as a sign that all would be as it should. Darkness fell upon her soul as the axe came rushing down.

*   *   *

Edgar walked into the house that stood near the barn. His hand had a large gash in it; blood dripped and left a trail on the clean white ceramic floors. He rushed to the kitchen, where his wife was standing at the sink. Upon hearing him return, she asked: "So, are they all dead?" Edgar, distracted by the cut on his hand simply replied "Yup."

Freda turned to face her husband and her eyes grew wide. "You're getting blood all over the place! Get over the sink. What in the bloody hell happened?" Edgar winced as the cold tap water began to clean the cut. Freda handed him a towel and said: "You better get that taken care of before it gets infected."

Edgar nodded and replied "I will, as soon as I finish what I started. I need to make room for the new chicks. We need the eggs." Freda started cleaning the blood on the kitchen floor as she said: "Bring me one of those chickens when you're done. We can have some stew for lunch."

HENRY

The dark blue mountain bike that Alex Billingsworth was riding whizzed past the majestic oak trees that lined the green near the waterfront. Across the bay, Oakwood Island could be seen through the hazy summer air. It was a hot August afternoon in the town of Anchor's Point, and only a slight warm breeze carried off the water and onto the mainland. Alex, a slim and meek teenager, decided to stop by Anchor's Point Park before he started his late shift at the hardware store that day.

Having been employed at the store as a general clerk meant that he was always the one being called on for errands and the small jobs that nobody else wanted. He had done cleanups, carry-outs and restocking since he was hired at the end of the school year, a few months prior. He liked his job. The money he made was spent on expanding his growing collection of vintage comics and cinema outings with his friends. As much as he liked his job, he felt the summer had gone by without much time for relaxation. To balance things out, Alex had been going to the park every week to meet up with the regulars that brought along their chess pieces to play on the chess-top tables in the park. About half a dozen of these tables adorned the green.

The players were mostly older gentlemen, longing for companionship and healthy competition. Alex had played most of the faces that gathered there just after lunch on weekdays. He knew which ones would try to distract him and slide a piece when he wasn't looking. He remembered who had grandchildren and who never talked of anything but the weather and the game. Yes, most faces he recognized and could predict his win or loss on the checkered tabletop.

As his bike neared the park, he slowed down a little, eyeballing the possible challengers. He saw that all the tables were occupied, and games were in progress. All tables, except for the furthest away, which sat square in the middle of the green, where no oak tree stood to provide shade and relief from the sweltering sun. As he made his way across the thin gravel path with his bike, through the green and between the trees, he recognized who sat at the sun-soaked table. As on every other hot day during summer, Henry could be found sitting at the most uncomfortable and sizzling table at the park.

The man was the only regular that Alex had yet to play, and he wasn't altogether sure that he wanted to either. Henry appeared to be in his mid to late seventies, based primarily on the lines and wrinkles that adorned his face. He consistently wore the same ragged clothes to the park. His deep brown leathery skin always moist with perspiration, the dark circles that seeped through the underarms of his off-white button down shirt seemed as fitting as the ketchup stain down the front pocket. The old man's brown fedora sat perched on his head, the edges frayed by years of use.

On the few occasions that Alex had seen him on the green, he had studied him with sympathetic curiosity. Henry was obviously a vagrant, or a drifter, usually sitting alone in the park. If someone happened on him and their eyes locked, he would grin widely and eagerly invite the passerby: "Play you for your soul," he would say in his deep and hoarse voice. Most people would walk away with a quickened step, smiling sympathetically, but uncomfortable with the old man's obvious mental state. His dark eyes would hold a stranger in a stare for what seemed like an eternity, and this was exactly what made many locals reject him.

Nobody really knew where Henry lived, or if he had any

family in Anchor's Point. One day he had just arrived in town, carrying his black velour bag that held his game pieces. Nobody talked of him, but exchanging glances with each other, the locals all knew what they needn't say out loud. The game of chess seemed to be the only true friend that Henry had found in Anchor's Point.

Alex slowed down as he approached the middle of the green, near the centre table where Henry sat. The old man's eyes traced the path from which the young boy had made his entrance. He cocked his head downward and to the right, his eyes peering over the rims of his glasses, staring intently at Alex as he brought his bike to a complete stop. Alex inexplicably had a shiver run up his spine, even though his work shirt was starting to get damp in this record-breaking heat wave.

Alex stood over his bike, examining the old man, trying to somehow uncover the dark secrets that lay behind those intense eyes. What caught his attention were the game pieces that Henry was setting out on the table. Black, hand-carved pieces lined up in two equal rows on Henry's side of the board. Ignoring a slight hesitation from within, Alex stepped down from the bike and started walking towards the centre table, every fibre in his body warning him to turn back, hop on his bike and just go to the local pool, where he could eye some pretty girls in bikinis before heading over to the hardware store to start his shift. Instead, the old man's stare pulled him in. With a chuckle in his voice, he smiled through a mouthful of rotten, old yellow teeth and asked Alex the same question he'd asked so many others before, "Play you for your soul?"

Alex smiled back and nodding he replied with a sarcastic tone, "Sure buddy, let's set up my side of the board and we'll see if you can have it or not." The old man chuckled and brought out the white hand-carved chess pieces, lining them up one by one in their respective spots, perfectly spaced on the miniature royal courtyard that was the tabletop.

Once the board was set, the game started and the conversation ended. They laboured over every move, taking time to ponder the possible ones that were coming next. The sun penetrated the pair's space, moving ever so slowly, casting shadows alongside the pieces, growing longer with each passing minute. The game seemed to make time stand still, each move longer than the prior, an indication of both their strong skill of play. Alex was a bit surprised that Henry was this good. He had thought him to be disturbed, but it became obvious with his adept moves on the board that this wasn't his first go round. "Where did you learn to play a board like this, mister?" Alex asked Henry. The old man's eyes transformed into dark slits as he smiled at his young opponent. "Don't ask questions that you don't want answered young man." He stared at Alex with those deep, dark eyes, making the boy uneasy.

Eventually, the few remaining pieces on the board set out to be in Henry's favour, and Alex swallowed hard before he said "Well I guess you win today. I can't believe you beat me old man, but you did." Henry grinned again, his stare uncomfortable. "I have to get to work now, mister. Thanks for the game." As Alex began to get up from the table, Henry reached across to collect the pieces of the game, but not before brushing the young mans' hand with his own. An electrifying sensation came over Alex in the instant the man's hand touched his.

The old man stared intently as Alex inexplicably became agitated and anxious. He backed away slowly, unsure of exactly why his heart had begun racing and his breathing had become rapid. He turned and grabbed his bike with both hands, jumping on it and pedalling off as fast as his skinny legs would allow, not looking back even once, for fear that Henry would be following him. Feeling the man's eyes on the back of his head was enough confirmation to Alex that he would not be accepting any more chess challenges from this fellow.

Although it was very hot that day, Alex felt his body become unnaturally hot as he made his way toward the hardware store. He didn't feel ill, but he was starting to burn up. Wiping the beads of sweat that formed on his forehead with the back of his hand, he felt the red-hot heat emanating from his skin. He could feel a few blisters forming, even though he had been wearing his ball cap. He knew for certain that this was no sun burn. He kept riding towards the store. His shift soon to start, he rode his bike as fast as he could.

While he made his way towards the centre of town, he tried to replay the moves of the game he'd just lost against old Henry. He rarely lost a game. He'd been to plenty of regional and even provincial tournaments and won most of them. When he did lose a game, which wasn't often, he retraced the moves to see where he'd gone wrong. He obsessively went through it in his head, his legs pumping to keep moving as fast as he could. With his thoughts on the game and the increasing heat spreading throughout his body, Alex never noticed the delivery truck making the left turn onto Water Street just as he was cruising down in that direction.

*   *   *

Bill was making his usual Tuesday afternoon delivery run to the hardware store. He had rolled down his windows, the breeze flowing in. He enjoyed the trip to Anchor's Point, as he loved the smell of the sea. Following the green near the waterfront, he made his way down the road. At the regular sight of sunbathers, dog walkers and chess players in the park, Bill smiled and drove on. Just as he was about to turn onto Water Street, he noticed an old black man standing on the outer edge of the green, with his long outstretched arm waving an old brown fedora. Bill felt a knot in his stomach, though unsure why, he waved back. The old black man grinned widely, with a strange look on his face, then placed his brown hat back onto his head. As soon as Bill set his eyes on the road again, turning onto Water Street, he saw what he could not avoid. The teen's eyes were as wide with shock as his own.

Bill, stunned, slammed on the brakes hard, but it was too late. Alex's bike smashed into it, his body hitting the truck with a powerful force, bones crunching on impact. As the driver came out running, he yelled over to the gathering onlookers to call 9-1-1. Across the street, still standing on the green in his dirty white button down shirt, the black man stood watching. Bill called out to the stranger, a lump forming in his throat: "I never saw him, I swear."

The old man nodded with a smirk and whispered "I know Bill, I know."

Looking down at Alex's contorted limbs and bloody torso, Bill swallowed hard.

He was in disbelief of what he was seeing. This young man had greeted him often at the hardware store when he had brought deliveries. He recognized him only by the green and yellow polo uniform shirt with the name "Alex" on the name tag. The only difference now was that the tag belonged to a battered young man instead of the vibrant and energetic one that had opened the door to him every Tuesday all summer long.

Bill looked up again to call the old man over to help him move the tangled metal off of the teen's legs, but the old man was nowhere to be seen. The green was empty of people now. Every last one of them had rushed alongside the road to see what had happened. The old man seemed to have simply vanished into thin air. Bill looked down again as Alex gurgled, his own blood starting to slowly drown him from within.

*　　*　　*

Alex, though still conscious, was only aware of one sensation, and that was the heat that grew stronger and hotter from within. His eyes staring up at the blue sky and the brightness of the afternoon sun, he felt his boiling blood pumping through his veins. Then, the sensation seemed to ease up and the world went dark around him.

When the ambulance arrived a few short minutes following the accident, Alex was hardly recognizable. Severe blisters covered his face and his broken body. It was obvious he had died of his injuries due to the impact of the truck, but it was unclear to everyone however, how the blisters had formed. Looking at him, the paramedics assumed he'd suffered burn injuries, but they couldn't make sense of why he'd been riding his bike if this was the case. They closed his inanimate eyes and covered his body with a blanket, while people watched with morbid curiosity the scene of the accident on Water Street.

*   *   *

Across the street, past the crowd and the green, below the boardwalk and onto the shore, there were a set of footprints in the damp sand. Each one deeply imprinted, they walked straight out from the bottom step of the wooden boardwalk and towards the water.

Henry stood there with his head cocked to the side as if listening. His eyes squinting, not from sweat or the sun, but as if focused on something.

"I did what you asked of me. I got you Alex before he could redeem himself. That's the third one I've given you," spoke Henry. He seemed to listen some more, then nodded... "Yes Masta. Three more souls and you will do for me what you says you would." He nodded as if to himself. "Three more and you give me mine."

Henry turned towards the churning waters of the sea, the bag containing the chess pieces slipping from his wrinkly hand. No longer needed, he let the pieces go. The pieces that had formed the royal battalion earlier, wooden kings and queens, knights and rooks, and small pawns danced together merrily on the open sea towards Oakwood Island.

Nodding as if in agreement, Henry spoke. "Yes Masta, take me to the next one." He walked towards the water but before he reached the sea however, he slowly faded away until he completely disappeared. Where the foam of the swaying waves formed, several small pieces of black and white floated with the current.

THE GIRL FROM IDLEWOOD

The night sky was clustered with large, dense clouds, their layers overlapping into each other, frolicking with the wind in one large mass. They passed over the full moon, their outlines bright, filtering the moonlight as they cast deep and dark shadows on the quiet back road. The trees still had a thick foliage that covered their quivering branches. Soon the foliage would completely transform into a myriad of colours and one by one the leaves would descend upon the dirt road below.

Darkness cloaked the tree-lined road, not sparing a single living thing from being drenched by the shadows. A porcupine gazed about in the middle of the road, pondering which direction to take next. Under its delicate paws, it felt a vibration that it recognized at once. Its eyes peered straight ahead for a moment until its natural instinct for flight took hold and it hurried across the road, into the ditch. It hid in the long overgrown grass and weeds that draped over the sides of the country path, like a bed skirt on a freshly made bed. The porcupine sensed the vibration approaching, and then it heard the rattling of the metal carcass and the humming of the electronic energy that the large creature emitted. The porcupine ran further still, away from the road, disappearing into the dark forest.

The road was nicknamed Idlewood Pass by residents of Clarkston at one end, and Clarkston Pass by residents of

Idlewood at the other. It was a long dirt road, void of life, except for the animals that called the surrounding woods their home. The Old Mill Road crossed its path at the midpoint between the two towns. Very rarely would this intersection see any kind of traffic, especially not this late at night.

Now, careening down the pass, on route towards Idlewood, came an old dark green 1966 Dodge Charger. It passed the spot where the porcupine had stood so still and quiet. With the headlights off, it swerved back and forth in the darkness of this stretch of road, sometimes missing the ditch by mere inches as it swerved back onto course, leaving a dusty trail behind. Small, pale hands clutched the steering wheel with a steel grip as they maneuvered the car in swift, jagged movements. A young woman sat in the driver's seat. She appeared to be in her early twenties. Her slim and svelte body leaned forward in the seat, while her eyes struggled to remain open and focused on the road. Her long and wavy dark brown hair cascaded down past her shoulders. Her eyes, which closed longer than they remained opened now, were of a deep green color. These pretty and innocent eyes struggled to stay awake, their beauty cloaked by the heaviness of their eyelids. The young woman passed out just as the old, beat-up Charger approached the Old Mill Road intersection.

*　　*　　*

The country music blaring from the old Ford truck shattered the silence of the night. Travelling on the Old Mill Road, the Jenkins boys were all crammed into Carl's old blue and white pick up. As the truck approached the intersection, the driver gasped as a dark shadow appeared directly in front of the truck's headlights. A dark car with no headlights on had cut directly in front of them at full speed. Carl only saw the car at the last second, and without any hint of the car's presence by sign of headlights, he had nearly hit the driver's door with full force.

He'd turned the steering wheel a quick and dramatic left, nearly rolling the truck as they were going so fast themselves. The truck came to a grinding stop in a cloud of dust in the middle of the intersection. The voice of the country singer wafted out through the opened windows of the truck and into the dark night air, mixing together with the dirt and grime that welcomed the twangy tune. Finally, as the dust settled around the truck, voices could be heard atop the music.

"Hoooooooooooo...that was close!" called out one voice.

"Fuck...spilled my beer," said another.

"What the hell!? Who the fuck is stupid enough to drive through here with no fucking lights on," said a third voice.

One at a time, three men stepped out of the truck. The driver, Carl, jumped out, slamming his door shut and spat on the ground next to his pickup. His anger was obvious as he walked around to the front of his truck, and looked up ahead to see if he could spot the car that he'd nearly crashed into just moments prior.

Stuart, who was Carl's younger brother, got out of the truck on the passenger side and flung his now empty beer bottle into the woods, making it clang against a tree. Thomas was the last out of the truck. Tom, as he was nicknamed, was also a Jenkins, but he was a cousin on their dad's side of the family. Following Stuart's lead (or Stewey as the older boys called him), he also flung his empty beer bottle into the woods and headed off to the front of the truck where Carl stood. Eventually, it was Stewey that spotted the car. He called out: "Look, the car's over there!"

The three of them made their way over to the car that had gone off the road and was now sitting lonely in the ditch. Their shuffling work boots made the dust rise up, illuminated by the rays of the truck's headlights, shining on them as they walked towards the immobilized car. As they got closer to the vehicle, Tom was the first to recognize it. "I know that car. Ain't no other Chargers like that one around here, not with that shitty patchwork!"

Carl stomped over to the car, his boots kicking some loose rocks and flinging them on the side of the green car. "You better have some fight left in ya, prick!" he yelled out as he got to door, his large and dirty hands grabbing the handle. His heart racing from anger he yanked open the door with brute force and bent over to grab the careless driver of the green Charger.

"Get him out of there, Carl. Bring him over here, and we'll do a number on him too!" Stewey called out from behind the ditched car.

Bending down to look at the driver, Carl's face went from angry to bewildered confusion. "What the fuck!? Hey bitch....wake up! You almost killed us back there!" Slumped over in the driver's seat was a young woman, her small frame covering not even half of the large steering wheel that her body pressed up against. She was facing Carl, her long brown hair covering most of her face. It was obvious that she was passed out cold. Carl called out to the other Jenkins and waved them over. "Ya gotta come see this!"

Tom and Stuart walked around to the side of the car where Carl was now standing with his hands on his hips. His anger had now turned into amusement as he admired the young girl, her long legs stretched out, her skirt just high enough for him to get an eyeful of her thighs. "That's one nice piece right there," he said as the other two men peered inside the car.

Tom bent down and spotted the faded black and white fuzzy dice hanging from the Charger's rear-view mirror. "I know her. She's that girl from Idlewood who works at the Clarkston liquor store. I'd recognize those long brown curls anywhere!" His hand moved a few strands of her hair out of her face to get a better look at the pale sleeping beauty.

Carl nudged the girl, trying to wake her up. "Hey, wake up! You can't be drinking and driving, didn't ya know?" Stewey and Tom burst out laughing, their own drunken state obvious.

"She's passed out, stone cold drunk she is," said Carl as he reached in and started to pull her out of the car. "Fuck this, guys. Let's take her back to the cabin. I bet we can teach her a lesson about getting drunk and having some fun with the boys!"

As Carl pulled her limp body out of the Charger, her legs still inside the car, Tom got in closer and carried her feet. "That little bitch wouldn't even look at me last night when I was buying beer. Stuck up one she is."

Tom and Carl lifted her up and out of the ditch. While they carried her towards the truck, Stuart ran ahead of them and jumped in the box of the pickup. He pushed aside the tools and the greasy fluid bottles that littered the box. Her arms dangled down as her body was clumsily carried by the two large men.

They crossed the headlights of the truck again, dust clouds rising up to the young girl's back and legs. She coughed dryly with her eyes still closed as the dust got into her nostrils and mouth. As they approached the truck, Stewey pulled open a large tarp and spread it across the box of the truck. They lifted her up onto the open tailgate and Stewey dragged her onto the tarp.

"Ya coming, turd?" Carl asked Stuart.

"Don't call me turd, dip shit. And no, I'm gonna stay here and make sure she doesn't try to jump off if she wakes up."

Carl rolled his eyes at his younger brother's obvious state of obsession with the young girl and headed back to the front of the truck. As he slammed the driver's side door shut, Tom picked up a cold bottle of beer from the case at his feet.

Drops of cold condensation stained his old faded blue jeans, as he brought the long neck to his mouth and gulped down a long swig of the cold brew. He handed a bottle to Carl and they joked about how they had started the night with bad luck at the pool hall but somehow lady luck had found them on this dark dirt road.

As the truck's massive engine revved the box of the truck vibrated and the girl moaned and stirred a bit. Stewey put a hand on her shoulder, and smiled down at her. His short stubby fingers pulled down the girl's light jacket that had ridden up to her waist when he'd dragged her into the truck's box. His gaze moved down to her bare legs, where her knee-length skirt was now hiked up to her mid-thighs. He rubbed her shoulder unconsciously. He glanced at the small curve of her breasts under her tight jacket and bending down he whispered in her ear, "Tonight, I'll give ya what ya always needed baby."

*   *   *

As the massive truck made its way down the dirt road, the young girl managed to open her eyes for a few brief moments. Her head got dizzy as soon as she saw the tree branches overhead, with the dark outlines of clouds in the backdrop. Confused, she wondered where she was. The last thing she remembered she had been in her car, trying to keep her eyes on the road. Her thoughts were unfocused, zooming in and out, just as fast as she was now zooming down the road. She could feel someone touching her shoulder. She struggled to open her eyes again, her lids heavy. She managed to open one eye and peer to her left. A man was sitting next to her. He smiled down at her and said something as his hand moved closer to touch her left breast. The loud roar of the engine muffled what he had said. Her mind screamed out for him to stop but her body, so weak and without energy, did not react in the least.

The last thing she saw before she closed her eyes again was the flash of a bright red light, then everything went black. She passed out again to the sound of the steady and loud pounding of each heartbeat, echoing in her head.

The truck that carried her groaned in an almost mocking fashion as it hit a pothole and shook her body. The truck was the first to violate her tonight, but it certainly would not be the last.

*   *   *

Carl turned off of Old Mill Road onto a bumpy and hardly visible trail. If not for the two thin dirt tracks in the grass, he could have easily gone off the road and ended up getting stuck out here in the boonies. With no cell tower for miles, there would have been no way of calling for help either. It would be a long walk back to Clarkston, so he tried to keep the truck as steady as he could as he made his way up the makeshift driveway.

After a few minutes, there came a clearing in the woods and the cabin came into view. It wasn't much to look at anymore. When the Jenkins brothers were young, their parents had kept the cabin well-maintained. Their mother had always kept it clean and organized, everything in its place. After she passed away when they were teenagers, and their father took to the bottle, the cabin had become a dark place. Darkness had pierced through not only the walls and floors of the cabin, but it had also seeped into the boys' lives.

Their father passed a few years after their mother, and so the cabin was now theirs. They lived in Clarkston in a cheap apartment, but they came to the cabin to drink on most weekends. As the headlights approached the old place, it was clear they hadn't inherited their mother's appreciation for cleanliness.

The front porch sank lower on the one side. The paint on the wooden siding was cracked and peeled. The window shutters were, for the most part, loose and about to fall off. The large bay window that had once been the prominent source of light in the boys' childhood was now cracked from top to bottom, the result of a beer bottle thrown in a fit of rage one night a few years back. It wasn't much to look at now, but Carl, Stuart and Thomas all filed out of the truck in hurried anticipation.

The young woman with the nice legs started rustling about when Tom slammed his door shut. Stuart was about to start towards the cabin when Carl yelled out to him, "Stewey, help me carry her inside, will ya!?"

Stuart turned around and glanced in the box of the truck as he came back. "Fuck off, Carl. I told you to stop calling me that you prick!" Stuart fidgeted with the zipper on his vest, trying to get it up. He peered back down at the girl, who was still passed out, but stirring on the tarp. Carl's laugh punctured the quiet of the deep woods, and he teased his younger brother, as he had always done since they were kids. "You're cute when you're mad, little Stewey."

His younger brother cursed under his breath and pulled the tarp down onto the tailgate. Carl bent down a bit and looked up the girl's skirt. "We got us a hot one tonight boys!"

Stuart climbed into the box again and picked up the woman under her arms as Carl carried her legs. As they lifted her off the truck, her small and delicate voice whispered, "Where am I?"

Carl's grin widened, and he gripped his hands tightly around her calves as he answered, "Why, you're at the Jenkin's love shack, and you're gonna get the royal treatment tonight!" The three Jenkins erupted in drunken laughter as they made their way up to the cabin's front porch steps. Carl turned to face Tom who was trailing behind him and said, "Tom, you go get some firewood!"

Tom stared at Carl for a brief moment and was about to protest when he realized that there was no use. Carl always got his way, no matter what. He turned and headed out down the trail that lead to the wood pile.

The two brothers carried the woman inside. The cabin was dark, as no electricity ran through these parts. Carl turned on the battery-operated lamp at the entrance, so they could see where they were going. There was a stench of stale alcohol and old overflowing ashtrays mixed in with the pungent odour of the uncleaned bathroom. Empty beer and liquor bottles littered the counter tops and table. Several food containers and grease-stained brown paper bags from the Clarkston takeout were strewn about on the floor and coffee table. "Shit, guess the maid didn't show up again!" Stuart joked.

Carl and Stuart made their way to the largest of the bedrooms, where their dead parents' bed still stood, void of blankets. It only had an old soiled sheet that was ripped down one side. They plopped the woman with the long brown hair onto the bed. Carl turned on the kerosene lamp near the bed while Stuart pushed her up higher. Her skirt moved up to her thighs and her pink lace-lined cotton panties were exposed.

Both men stared for a long moment. Carl broke the silence as he unbuckled his belt. "Go have a beer, Stewey. I'll let ya know when I'm done with her."

Stuart stared at his brother. He opened his mouth to protest just as Carl turned his back to him and pulled the woman's legs down again, letting them dangle over the edge of the bed. Stuart knew it was useless to argue with his bully of a brother. He always got his way, and was always first. Stuart closed the door behind him as he heard his brother's belt buckle hit the wooden floor boards.

*   *   *

The pile of firewood was a good walk away from the cabin. It had been the brothers who had hauled and split it a few months back, so now it was always Tom's job to go fetch the firewood. This was a job that Tom despised, as he never got to start in on the fun with the brothers. He was always the last one to join in. He grumbled and cursed as he walked down the path from the side of the cabin, over to the small tool shed. The wood pile sat in the dark in front of the shed. Tom started filling the red wheelbarrow with firewood, making sure to fill it. He figured he didn't want to keep running out here all night, so he would bring plenty to save himself some trips later on tonight.

As he grabbed a large piece near the bottom of the pile, he felt a sharp prickling sensation. "Ow, fuck!" he yelled out. A large splinter had pierced the skin just below his thumb and a small blood drop formed instantly. He brought his hand to his mouth and sucked at the blood and splinter. His teeth found the edge of the small wooden weapon and he pulled it out of his hand. "What a fuckin' night this is starting to be," he grumbled. The old wheelbarrow tipped over as he flung the next piece in too fast and all the other pieces fell out. Tom stared and shook his head. What a fuckin' night indeed.

*   *   *

Stuart stormed out of the dark cabin by way of the back door. He fumed and cursed at himself for not standing up to Carl. All his life he'd been bullied by his older brother, and never dared to stand up to him. On the few occasions he'd tried getting up the nerve, he'd chickened out when Carl glared at him, his hands forming into large fists of fury. He knew better than to upset Carl. Upsetting Carl would mean he'd get a pounding.

Stuart walked out into the night and headed for the generator. It wasn't always easy getting the old clunker going. Ever since Carl accidentally put kerosene in the tank during one of his drunken moments, the old generator hadn't worked right since.

Stuart got the small gas canister on the side of the generator and started working on it. He had to keep himself occupied to keep his mind off Carl and the girl that he had wanted a go at first. He'd been eyeing her ever since she started working at the liquor store earlier in the month. Now his brother was gonna have her first. He slammed the canister of gas on the ground and cranked the generator over and over again, trying to get it started.

*   *   *

The bedroom was dark except for the dimly lit lantern on the side table near the bed. Carl started touching the young woman, and as he did so she started stirring and moaning, still unconscious. "I wish you'd wake up bitch. I prefer a fight from whores like you!" He took a long swig of the beer he'd picked up on his way in the cabin, and started to have his way with her.

After a few moments, the young woman began to rouse and move about. "Oh, yeah baby, that's it, you're feeling me now, aren't ya?"

Carl's large hands were holding down her hips when she grabbed them with her own small, cold and wiry hands. Carl looked at her at once, his excitement rising as he felt her struggling body beneath him. Her eyes were rolling back in her head now, and Carl knew this was in no way a good thing.

Her back arched wide in a violent fashion as she let out an uncanny moan, much louder and stronger than a body this size could possibly let out. The woman thrashed her head to one side, whipped her hair out of her face and let it fall back down on the soiled bed. Carl's eyes spread wide and fearful as he noticed two large puncture marks on her neck. Bright red blood now trickled from each hole and down into her cleavage that Carl had so openly admired just moments before. She jerked her head up and brought it within inches of his face, flashing her long, white canines at him. Her hot and putrid breath now hissed onto his face.

As Stuart finally got the generator going outside, the roar of the machinery filled the quietness of the night, and the lights inside the cabin came on all at once. Carl looked on in drunken and frightful stupor at the pale and emotionless face that was inches from his own. Her legs that had been limp and hanging over the bed only moments before were now wrapped tightly around his own, her inhuman strength crushing him. She wrapped her small arms around him, and as he tried to push her away, he found he was now the weak one, her grip like iron. She bit down hard and urgently, his blood oozing out from the small punctures her teeth left in his neck, her hunger taking over her as she greedily took in every last drop of his scarlet essence.

Carl tried to scream but only a whimper came out as she drained him. The generator steadily hummed along, muffling his pitiful cries for help. His body fell to the floor, crumpling under her small body. The young woman's hunger for blood was only partially satiated. She also craved the taste of revenge. As the door to the room began opening, her dark and angry eyes stared wildly at what was coming next.

*   *   *

Stuart came in through the back door, having finally calmed himself enough to come back inside. He would be second in line to have his way with the little tease, always smiling at him when he went through her cash register. He knew she wanted him most anyways, so she wouldn't mind waiting for him he thought to himself as he put the rest of the beer away in the fridge.

As he was putting away the last few bottles, he heard a loud thump coming from the bedroom followed by a groaning sound. "Carl, ya alright in there? Ya ain't banging her up too much I hope. Save some of that pretty ass for me." Stuart started to make his way towards the bedroom door, a beer in hand. He cracked open the new bottle of brew and flung the cap across the kitchen floor. He heard another groan. This time it sounded like his brother, but not his usual self.

Curious, Stuart approached the bedroom door and opened it slowly. Shock swept over him as he looked at the scene before him, dropping the beer bottle to the floorboards, and sending bits and pieces of brown glass and the foamy brew in all directions. Carl was sprawled out on his back on the floor at the foot of the old bed. The young woman was straddled atop of him, hunched down with her head cradled in his neck, her wild eyes staring Stuart down.

The single overhead bulb shone a bright and hard light down onto the pair. As Stuart began to tremble, she got up on her feet and hissed, splattering Carl's blood into the air as her long teeth protruded out of her mouth. Stuart noticed the puncture marks on his dead brother's neck and looked up at the girl, her bloody mouth proof of what had just occurred. "Fuck me! Vampires don't exist!" he exclaimed, starting to back away from the bedroom.

In a nearly inaudible and soft tone of voice, the young woman replied "I would have said the same thing a few hours ago." With this said, she pounced with such speed and force onto Stuart's chest that he never had time to process what was happening.

Never having expected such a powerful force from this tiny woman, he staggered back a few clumsy steps. The struggle only lasted but a brief moment, his face as pale as hers in fear of what was about to become of him. She forced his head in an unnatural motion, snapping his neck with such force that he slumped to the floor with her on top of him. At once her sharp teeth punctured his still warm neck, the pulsing of his aorta growing weaker and weaker as the blood flow now poured into her mouth.

*   *   *

The night sky had cleared up nicely by the time Tom had gathered up the second load of firewood into the wheelbarrow. He looked upwards at the hundreds upon hundreds of stars and the full moon that shone with all its might. The path now well lit for his walk back towards the cabin, Tom pushed the wheelbarrow steadily, determined to finally join in on the fun inside the cabin. He kept muttering to himself as he went along, still fuming that he was always the one having to collect firewood. Carl had insisted on having the wood pile as far away from the cabin as possible. "Tough guy, afraid of snakes in the wood pile. Maybe he ain't that tough after all."

As he kept muttering to himself, his foot brushed up against something on the ground near the truck. Tom let go of the wheelbarrow and turned around to see what he had stepped on. Crouching down, he picked up a small wallet, dirty from the dust in the driveway. Having wiped away most of the dirt, he opened it. He assumed it was the young woman's and that it must have fallen out of her jacket when the brothers carried her out of the truck.

Tom flipped through it, not finding much of anything. Thirty-eight bucks, a few receipts, and her photo ID card. He looked over the card and said aloud, "Marlee, huh? So that's your name. Can't wait to have my fun with you bitch. Oh, you're gonna scream for me tonight." He stood and started back up towards the cabin. As his eyes glanced upwards, he stopped dead in his tracks.

Standing on the front porch a few yards away was the tiny woman the brothers had carried into the cabin not so long ago. Her face was contorted into a deranged grin; her cheeks and chin were blood-covered, dripping down onto her opened white jacket and tank top underneath. Her hair even seemed matted with a thick coating of dark liquid. No doubt more blood. As the breeze made the leaves shiver, it also carried with it a distinctive aroma. Marlee picked up on the smell and her eyes narrowed as they fixated on the man she had been about to feast upon. She sensed something different about this man, something that she hadn't sensed from the other two. She dared not feed on him, but she had other plans for him.

She smiled at Tom from up the porch steps and exclaimed, "Who's gonna scream for who, bitch!?"

Tom dropped the wallet and its contents on the ground and turned to run away. He hardly had time to take half a step before Marlee was on the ground, her force multiplied from her recent feedings. As her small body rushed and tackled the last of her abductors from behind, the impact snapped his back instantly. His back broken, the blow sent him flying through the air, some twenty feet down the driveway, where he bounced like a rag doll before coming to an abrupt stop in the dirt. Tom's body lay contorted in the driveway in a grotesque position. Both his legs were spread out to one side, his feet nearly touching his upper thighs.

He felt no pain. He noticed the dirt rising into his nostrils with each breath he inhaled. When he tried to lift his head, he realized his body wouldn't budge. Marlee stood where he had just been a few seconds earlier, laughing mercilessly at his predicament. He watched her as she slowly turned and made her way to the old Ford truck. The keys in the ignition as they always were, the young woman powered up the engine and Tom felt the vibrations of the truck's powerful engine on his cheek, which was involuntarily pressed against the driveway's dirt. Tom looked on, horrified, as the young woman put the truck in gear and made a quick U-turn in the driveway. The headlights now shone directly into Tom's face, blinding him temporarily. He closed his eyes.

The truck was a good thirty yards away from him, but he felt the vibrations on his cheek growing as steadily as the fear that welled up in the pit of his stomach. She started towards him, the truck slowly inching closer. The anger that had build up inside the young woman's body rose up and exploded outwards as she uttered a long wild scream of agony. Her foot pressed hard on the gas of the old Ford and up it came at full speed towards Tom. Panic and horror filled his very soul, but he was unable to move. When the smell of the tires wafted into his nostrils, he closed his eyes as hard as he possibly could, and for a split second, the crunching sound of his skull collapsing unto itself under the weight of the truck's tire resonated into his ears.

*   *   *

Driving down Idlewood Pass, there came an old blue and white Ford pickup truck. It passed a porcupine that was crouched in some bushes on the side of the road. The full moon hung overhead, casting a veil of light that shone on the face of the lone occupant. So small was the young lady that drove the truck, she was barely able to see over the steering wheel.

Marlee, a tiny young thing, had originally been from Idlewood. She had graduated this past year from Idlewood High, and had started working at the Clarkston Liquor Store recently to help her mother pay the mortgage. She had been a quiet girl, shy and reclusive. Her cats had been her closest friends throughout her childhood. She had held a deep appreciation for animals and had never hurt a living thing in her life, until tonight. The new, blood-seeking Marlee held absolutely no compassion for any living thing. She couldn't afford to anymore as compassion might mean her death and the need to feed would prove too strong. Her mind was foggy and her memory of that day a haze. She could not remember whom had done this to her. She tried hard to remember and mere bits came back in flashes. Blind with rage she drove wanting revenge. She felt her body become stronger after having just fed. Her senses too grew sharper. Somehow she knew her memory would follow, she would be able to remember where and how it had happened to her. This curse that seemed fiction not long ago, stuff of movies and books.

The truck revved up faster as she felt the strength well up inside her. A trail of dust and rocks spat out from behind the truck.

The porcupine ran back into the deep woods to hide from the metal monster that carried the night predator away into the darkness.

ABOUT THE AUTHORS

Angella Jacob grew up in St. Antoine, New Brunswick where she developed an interest for reading and writing from a very young age. Her curious nature about everything paranormal and mysterious carved the inspiration for her current passion of writing horror and mystery stories. Angella is a mother of two boys and also a freelance graphic artist.

Pierre C Arseneault grew up in Rogersville, New Brunswick, where his strong imagination helped form the creative individual he is today. Pierre has been published as a freelance cartoonist, publishing in newspapers since 2004.

Dark Tales for Dark Nights is the first print publication that the pair of collaborative writers have made available for their readers. Both authors currently reside in the greater Moncton area of New Brunswick, Canada.